Didgeridoo

Other books by Binkey Kok Publications

Eva Rudy Jansen
Singing Bowls
A practical Handbook of Instruction and Use

Eva Rudy Jansen
The Book of Buddhas
Ritual Symbolism used
on Buddhist Statuary and Ritual Objects

Eva Rudy Jansen
The Book of Hindu Imagery
The Gods and their Symbols

Ab Williams
The Complete Book of Chinese Health Balls
Background and Use of the Health Balls

George Hulskramer
The Life of Buddha
Prince Siddharta to Buddha

Töm Klöwer
The Joy of Drumming
Drums and Percussion Instruments from around the World

Dirk Schellberg

Didgeridoo

Ritual Origins and
Playing Techniques

Binkey Kok Publications, Havelte, Holland

CIP-DATA KONINKLIJKE BIBLIOTHEEK, DEN HAAG

Schellberg, Dirk

Didgeridoo, Ritual Origins and Playing Techniques/Dirk Schellberg
[transl. from The German by Tony Langham ... et al.;
photographs & ill. Dirk Schellberg] - Diever: Binkey Kok - Ill., photo's.
Transl. of: Didgeridoo, Das faszinierende Instrument der australischen
Ureinwohner - Südergellersen: Verlag Bruno Martin GmbH 1993
ISBN 90-74597-13-0
Subject headings: Music.

Published and © by Binkey Kok Publications, Havelte, Holland.
Fax 00 31 521 591925

Printed and bound in the Netherlands.
Lay-out: Eva Rudy Jansen
Cover Design: Jaap Koning BnO

Distributed in the U.S.A. by
Samuel Weiser Inc., Box 612, York Beach, Maine 03910

Dedicated to

Ngaljod
the Rainbow Snake from the Dreamtime

Table of contents

Introduction

When I visited Australia for the first time in 1986, I was fulfilling a dream I had cherished for years. I travelled round hitchhiking or by bus, and sometimes I was on the road for 36 hours at a stretch. I would gaze at the landscape passing by for hours on end, though it always looked the same. And yet I never became bored – although there wasn't really anything to see. Or was there?

In the bush, looking for somewhere to shelter from an imminent thunderstorm, I found myself in a hut used as a resting place for travellers in the outback. Soaked through and bitterly cold, I was woken up the next morning by a load banging and clattering. An Aborigine was making breakfast for the group of tourists with whom he was travelling. He was in top form -how could he manage to be so jolly when the weather was so awful? But he knew what had happened outside: in the space of one night the bush had started to blossom!

I think that was the moment that my attention was drawn to the reality of the original inhabitants of Australia, and no longer merely to the aspects of folk lore.

From that moment it was obviously only a matter of time before I came across my first didgeridoo, and now that this wonderful instrument has resulted in a commission for writing this book, it is also that instrument which gives me the opportunity to write something about these original inhabitants.

When I started this book I intended to write only a short introduction about playing the didgeridoo, but my background research started to lead a life of its own and brought its own tales with it. That is why this book has finally become much more than merely a description of playing the instrument.

It all started when I was sitting by the open fire of Bruno Martin's house playing my didgeridoo, and he asked me whether I wouldn't like to write something on the subject of didgeridoos. I realized that he was serious when the publishing contract arrived in my letter box no more than three weeks later.

I am grateful to Bruno Martin for setting up this project, but there are many other people I would like to thank and I will mention them all here: Taimi Zaeske, who translated things for me; Peter Zaeske, who helped me with my problems in German; Nana Nauwald, who met me in Frankfurt with my 70 kilos of didgeridoos; Gabi Engert-Timmermann, who gave me my first lessons on the didgeridoo; and Jutta Haberhauer, who shed some light on the numerous theoretical problems which I encountered. Finally, there is D-Team Design, who lent me a computer.

I would also like to thank my friends in Australia, Louisa Miller and Elmar Wolters, for their hospitality and support. Thank-you, Denise Brewster and the Sunrize Band, who gave me an insight into the Australian music business. Bob Gosford provided me with a great deal of background information about the contemporary social conditions of the Yolngu. I would like to thank the members of the Wugularr community, whose life I shared for a while.

A special thanks to David Blanasi, who put up with me even though I have so much to learn about civilization. He taught me a great deal about life and, of course, about didgeridoos.

Foreword

As you read this book you will occasionally come across unfamiliar terms such as Koori, Anangu, Yolngu. I used these words as often as possible to replace the term Aborigine, which is usually used to describe the original inhabitants of Australia. Even in Australia itself it is increasingly common to use these terms which these people use themselves.

Koori, is the name of the original inhabitants of the south of Australia. The term Anangu is used particularly in Central Australia, and the term Yolngu is used in the north. These were the main areas where I travelled.

The didgeridoo is a traditional instrument played by men and is never really played by women. Undoubtedly there are traditional reasons for this. In my view, it is not absolutely necessary for us in the west to keep to these traditional rules.

The fact that I constantly refer in this book to the player as 'he' or 'his', certainly does not mean that I am writing only for men. However, our language still lends itself to this imbalance, and despite using the terms 'he' and 'his', I hope that women will feel that the book is also written for them. In fact, one of my very first lessons on the didgeridoo was from a woman!

Part 1

The Journey to the Didgeridoo

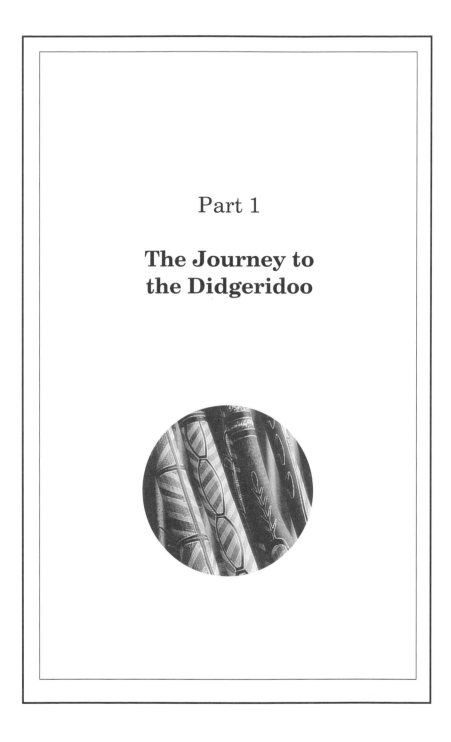

On the Road

Parallel lines cross at infinity. For some time this concept had been in my mind. By the side of an Australian highway in the Northern Territory the concept achieved a tangible reality for me. The black strip of asphalt stretched out in front of me in a straight line as far as the horizon. Blue sky, red sand, a sun which scorches everything around mercilessly: was this what I was looking for? I only became aware of the fact that my shadow was exactly underneath me when I realized that – curiously – there was no shadow.

It was January. At this time of year the sun was at an angle of 90 degrees above me and the temperature was approximately 32 degrees in the shade. These are certainly not the best conditions to be standing by the side of the road hitching a lift. The eighth or ninth 'Road Train' had just thundered past. Road Trains are gigantic lorries, sometimes with three trailers, which carry just about all the goods through the interior of Australia. With a normal pick-up truck you need quite a bit of time to overtake one of these monsters, which can be up to 50 metres long. Once they move, they do not brake for anything or anyone. That is why there is an indestructible rack mounted on the front to protect the motor, known as the so-called Bull or Roo Barn. The numerous corpses littering the roadside soon reveal the reason for these names.

An experienced traveller will know that when he is standing by a dirt road and the obligatory cloud of dust on the horizon heralds the approach of a Road Train, it's best for him to take cover. The grit thrown up by one of these monsters can be quite dangerous, particularly for windscreens. The part of the road where I was standing was asphalted, so that I could take advantage for a few seconds of the cooling stream of air accompanying the vehicle. The sun blazed on. I had not really wanted to hitchhike on this journey because I had not yet forgotten my experiences of my last voyage in Australia. I remembered some of the scenes from 1970s road movies of lonely hitchhikers by abandoned roads. But I was not there to write a 'road story'. The reason I had come back to Australia was leaning against my rucksack and looked like a long thick club. It was a didgeridoo. Superficially, a didgeridoo could be described as a thick branch hollowed out by termites, which is used by the original inhabitants of Australia as a wind instrument. However, that is a very superficial description.

I was making this journey because of this instrument, and it became a key which gave access to a number of very special encounters. I was on my way to Wugularr, an 'Aboriginal community' in the tropical north of Australia. These communities are villages or settlements where the Yolngu live. The term Yolngu (= people) is the term used by the Aborigines themselves in the north, who would like to be known as the 'original inhabitants' in their own country. The white colonists did not even take the trouble to call the Aborigines by their own name. It is not easy to establish contact with the Yolngu, particularly outside the tourist areas in one of the National Parks, such as for example, the Kakadu National Park. A white man needs written consent from the responsible Land Council to enter the Yolngu area. He must state his reason for going, and the duration of his stay. The Land Council is a sort of administrative organ, and there is one in every state. Since the Yolngu fought for their land rights in the 1970s (Landrights Acts), their territories are more or less private land. Obviously there is one proviso: in many cases it transpired that these areas which had been thought to be infertile and unprofitable, actually concealed valuable mineral deposits or could be exploited in another way, such as tourism. In those cases it soon became clear what these land rights actually meant. At best, the owners would be paid part of the profits.

I was fortunate to meet Johnny Lane, a Yolngu from whom I

bought my first didgeridoo in Australia. We became friends and even played together as street musicians; this is where the Australian term 'busking' comes from. Because he knew I wanted to write about didgeridoos, he said to me one day: 'If you really want to know anything about didgeridoos you must go and visit my father, David Blanasi? I will arrange it, no worries!' I was able to arrange permission for this visit on the telephone with the mayor of Wugularr. This was a good recommendation for the Land Council. I was to get a lift in a car which regularly transported goods to the area. But all my attempts to sort this out came to nothing. After waiting in Katherine for five days, I therefore decided to go on my own. Once I had hitchhiked to the crossroads where you had to leave the highway, someone would be bound to pass who would take me further.

I painted the English name of Wugularr on a sign (almost all the communities have an English name and a Yolngu name). However, I did not succeed in getting a single driver to stop. The whites were certainly suspicious, for what did a white man want from the 'Abos' out there in the bush? This enthusiastic view of the Yolngu certainly did not make them very popular everywhere. But I was a really suspicious character for the 'blackfellas'.

When I'd been standing by the road for hours with the sun beating down on my head, I decided to give myself exactly another half hour for that day. On the back of my sign I wrote the Yolngu name of Wugularr. Johnny had told me that name, thought it is hardly known and not shown on a single map. Perhaps that is why it inspired confidence, because fifteen minutes later someone offered me a lift. It was a land rover full of Yolngu. They offered to take me to another community quite close to Wugularr. I no longer cared so long as I got away from that spot – even if I had to spend the night out in the open – 'Go bush !' I crowded into the truck with the others. Half a dozen faces with grins stretched to their ears stared at me semi-timidly, though with some benevolent curiosity. The younger ones laughed, 'What was this tall 'whitefella' planning in the bush?'. They soon turned their attention to my yidaki (didgeridoo). Obviously the kids wanted to play it. It passed from one to the other and they all showed me what they could do – what I heard sounded frighteningly good. At last I was in the 'promised land'; I inwardly rejoiced. Unfortunately, the man sitting next to me, an older man, only spoke 'language', i.e., one of the many Yolngu dialects. However, I managed to understand that he had just come out of hospital. He was celebrating this by drinking one can of beer after another. Alcohol is prohibited in the community, and so he had to finish his supply before we arrived.

When we arrived at the settlement, it was a shock. It is true that I had read a great deal about the contemporary life of the Yolngu, but I had not really thought about what I would encounter in reality. The harshest description that I had ever read had compared one of these communities to Beirut after a rocket attack. In my eyes, the village made an utterly cheerless and dilapidated impression: neglected bungalows, wrecked cars and rubbish everywhere. If only I didn't have to get out. Were these my Dreamtime heroes with me as the carefree Dream dancer? My sense of joy was soon replaced by a deep feeling of oppression. I asked the driver whether they could drop me on the road to Wugularr, but they indicated that I should stay in the car. We drove through the village. At one of the bungalows they stopped to let out a few of the other travellers. A man came out of the house, and after exchanging a few words with the driver, he informed me that they had decided to take me to Wugularr straightaway. After all, it wouldn't be long until sunset. In order to get there quickly the man got behind the wheel immediately. And with an enormous dust cloud following the car like a flag, we tore along the dirt road.

It was a real test of endurance for cars. The vehicle bounced up and down so much that I had the feeling that I was floating above my seat, rather than sitting on it. What would Wugularr be like?

My first impression of this community was a lot better than that of the last one, but a new problem arose straightaway. How was I to find David Blanasi? Did he know that I was coming? All the arrangements I had tried to make recently had proved to be rather unreliable; so why should this one be allright? However, my worries were unfounded. The driver had dropped me at the guest house where David was living with his friend, Tom Kelly. In some way everyone knew that I was coming. There were children everywhere, curly headed, smiling broadly, white teeth, happy faces. David slowly came down the verandah. Later he told me that he had known for a few days about my arrival, though he had no idea who or what was coming. Dark eyes gazed at me rather anxiously and suspiciously – what did I want here? I did not really feel at ease. There were too many impressions to take in, too much unfamiliarity. Once again the didgeridoo served as a key, as a negotiating instrument. I told him that I had met his son in Darwin and that he had sent me to him because I was really keen to learn as much as possible about didgeridoos. I had been told that he, David Blanasi, was an authority on that field.

I only realized much later how true this was. After I had hauled my things onto the verandah and had told him the latest news about his son, he asked me: 'Do you know how to play it?' 'The basics', I answered, so that he wouldn't have too many expectations. I showed him my didge and he immediately started to knead the mouthpiece, making the opening significantly larger than I was used to. Then he passed the instrument back to me and said: 'O.K., let's have a try'. I put the didge to my lips and started to play. Slowly my nervousness ebbed away, the vibration took over my whole body and resulted in that special stimulating effect which I enjoy every time I play. After a few minutes I stopped. 'Allright'. David pronounced this word 'allright' in a way in which I have only heard from the Yolngu; it showed that he thought he could do something with me. This was the starting signal for ten very instructive days.

David lives in the former guest house. He has left his bungalow to his family, I think because this means he has more peace and quiet without the 'mob'. The mob is the word which is commonly used for the group, the mass. The Yolngu often call themselves the mob: 'Us mob, good mob', etc. In the south the Aborigines also call themselves 'Koori', and they insist that this

**The guest house with
unfinished didgeridoo pipes
in the foreground.**

name is also used for them in the media.
The guest house is built on stilts. The five adjacent rooms are
joined with a long verandah, which is a very important spot.
This is where the cooking is done, work is carried out and
visitors are welcomed. Among his own people, David is an
important person. He was born in 1930 near Katherine, and
belongs to the Miaili language group.
Following the Japanese air attack on Katherine, David had to
leave the area. He moved with his family to the present
settlement of Barunga. There he was elected to be taught the
traditional songs and to play the didgeridoo. He is familiar
with many ceremonies and has been on tour a number of times
abroad as an Australian cultural ambassador; Japan, Hawaii,
Mexico, Papua New Guinea, Israel and France are some of the
places which he has visited.
David has taught a number of white musicians to play the
didgeridoo , musicians who owe a considerable debt to the
didgeridoo in their careers, such as, for example, Rolf Harris,
Steven Cooney, Charley McMahon and Ted Egan. One of the
stories David likes to tell is about the time that Rolf Harris
'freed' him from jail in Katherine and brought him to Sydney
for the 'Walkabout' T.V. series. David Blanasi has been in many
documentary films, e.g., for the Australian Institute of Aboriginal Studies' in Canberra. Nowadays, David is invited by
very distant communities to initiate children into their own
culture, or to lead certain ceremonies which are partly secret,
and which are known to only a few initiates.
However, I did not know all this on that first evening. When I
arrived, a class of a schoolchildren from another community
had just visited David and Tom to learn songs and dances. I
now know that these men-of-knowledge are fighting an
important battle to give their people a cultural identity. But
they have some powerful opponents. The blessings of the white
culture have a great influence on the young Yolngu, who have to
survive in these two very different cultures.
If you really wanted to come to grips with the Yolngu culture, it
would take a whole lifetime to pass through the most important
initiation rituals. The history of the Yolngu has not been

recorded in writing. The past, the present, and the future are closely related to the land where the Yolngu live. Every spot has its own significance, and this is passed on orally in traditional stories.

When these people seem to be sitting lazily under a tree in the afternoon, they are often passing on history. This is an important part of daily life. The stories, which are known as 'Dreamings', have little to do with our definitions of dreams, despite the name. In fact, it is a highly active process, in which no distinction is made between the mythological and the everyday view of the world. In order to understand these complex structures, the Yolngu have to spend a large part of their time on spiritual matters. For us it is often difficult to gain an idea of the immaterial cultural wealth of the Yolngu. In their own language they often know more than 30,000 expressions ! Many of them only really speak English as their second or even third language. The most fantastic aspect of their perception is that which Barbara Gloczewski calls 'mythical social geography'. The history is actually contained in the land itself; if a Yolngu, an Anangu or Koori loses his connection with the land, he loses his origins. For an Aborigine, this means the loss of the earth on which he lives, in the same way that we would lose our history if we lost our libraries or data banks. This is why it was impossible for the Aborigines to move away from their land to make way for the colonists without losing their identity. Misunderstandings on both sides resulted in violence and inevitably the Aborigines always came off worse.

When you are with a Yolngu who really knows the bush, he will tell you that he reads the land. On the other hand, there are video games, alcohol abuse and glue sniffing. Without work and alienated from their own culture because of the whites' attempts to assimilate the Aborigines, many flee the hopeless, cheerless reality to seek refuge in artificial intoxication. It is only in the last twenty years that white Australians have acquired any idea of the great cultural heritage which is in the process of being lost.

At last there is a programme of aid being set up for the Yolngu which is not at the same time trying to dominate or patronise them.

At any rate, for the first time I witnessed a fairly active cultural heritage. The school class which I mentioned was spending its last evening in Wugularr. Before they left, there was a barbecue. I think David wanted to show me what he and Tom had taught the children, because they were asked to perform a dance. The children were obviously showing off a bit for the visitor, who had suddenly turned up. David later obstinately insisted that the dance had not been performed especially for me, but I didn't really believe him. Tom played the didgeridoo and David sang while he banged together a couple of clapsticks (also known as bilma). You could tell that they were proud of their work.

Originally didgeridoos were not solo instruments. They come from the musical context in which the focus is the 'song owner', who sings and beats time at the same time. There are accounts of songs which take weeks, and even months to be sung all the way through. The Ubar, one of the most important ceremonies in western Arnhemland, lasts for two to three weeks. In spiritual terms, this ceremony takes place at the bottom of the Milky Way. It deals with the processes of creation, fertility and growth. On these occasions there may be several singers, but only one didgeridoo is played.

Of course there are exceptions. For example, Keith Cole wrote about a funeral ceremony where four didgeridoos were played and the 'song-leader' sang and played the bilma for four hours on end.

David using the sander.

The Didgeridoo Factory

Life in Wugularr slowly gets going every day just after sunrise. We started the day with a gigantic pot of tea. For breakfast, David and the others drink at least a litre of tea. Often friends and members of the family came by for a chat and a cup of tea. Unfortunately, they spoke to each other in 'language', and I heard only the occasional bit of English. It was used only for concepts which do not occur in their own language, such as numbers, telling the time, or technical terms. The didgeridoos are boiled and manufactured on the verandah. There is a constant constructive chaos. David was working on painting a new pipe while Tom was sanding the trunks, the bark of which had already been removed with a sander; modern times even in the didgeridoo business. Most communities have electricity, even in the most remote parts of the bush. In order to show me the creation of a didgeridoo from the very beginning, David persuaded Bob to travel into the bush with a land rover to a place where the 'didgeridoo trees' literally grow all over the place. Bob is a white man who originally came from Darwin, where he is studying law. He does a lot of work with the Yolngu. At the time he was writing a treatise about the linguistic misunderstandings which apparently often occur in legal proceedings. Many English words have a completely different meaning for the Yolngu. About 1.4% of the total population of Australia is Aborigine; but in prisons this percentage is at least ten times higher.

There was a pick-up available for us from amongst the vehicles which belong to the community, and some of us sat in the trailer. A number of spare tyres and jacks were also put in the back.

It made sense that a number of other 'didgeridoo builders' joined our expedition, because it was a matter of building up the supply of didgeridoos. It was quite late in the morning and the sun was already scorching. For a 'whitefella', it's not much fun to take a trip in the trailer in these conditions. A hat, trousers, a long-sleeved shirt and sun cream with a factor 16 are essential, even when you think you are tanned enough to endure the rays of the sun. On the other hand, this way of travelling does give the whole exercise an authentic feel: you smell the smell of the earth, the red dust grates between your teeth and above all, there is the blue, blue sky, which I could have enjoyed forever.

As soon as we arrived at our destination, David jumped out of the car, took his axe and strode into the bush, full of determination. Before I realized what was happening, he had already gone quite a way ahead and I found it difficult to keep up. When you think of the 'bush', you shouldn't imagine any dense vegetation; it's more like the landscape in a park. The trees are fairly far apart, and in between the grass is knee-high and there are lots of low bushes. Some areas are covered with termite hills, red constructions like pillars about a metre tall. There are even some which reach a height of three to five metres.

Once you've lost sight of the road, it becomes difficult to orient yourself, because everything looks the same in every direction. Once the sun has reached its highest point, or if it's cloudy, it's not even possible to orient yourself by the sun. There are stories about people who went just a little too far from the road when they stopped to take a leak, and were then unable to find their car again. Once they are in the bush, the Yolngu become different creatures. In Wugulaar, I always had the feeling they couldn't live as they wanted to. But here in the wilderness which is familiar territory, they are completely spontaneous, omnipotent and wonderfully crazy and exuberant.

The trees which are suitable for making a didgeridoo must comply with certain requirements. They must be tall enough so that two pieces can be 'harvested', and they must have the right diameter. But the most important condition is they must be hollow ! The story that the trunks are placed in a termite hill so that they can be gnawed away is complete fabrication. Various different types of wood are used, depending on the region: yellow box gumtree, bloodwood, red river gum, stringy bark, woollybutt. These are all different varieties of eucalyptus (stringy bark = Eucalyptus tetodonta, woollybutt = Eucalyptus miniata) the trunk of which is hollowed out by termites while the tree continues to grow.

The trees which David chose were still alive. They were very slender, with a diameter of approximately 15 cm, and a height of 5 to 6 metres. Usually, you can't see that the trees are hollow from the outside. A small termite hill at the foot of the tree can be a good sign. In order to find out whether the trunk really was hollow, David peeled off a piece of the bark so that he could tap on it with his knuckles and hear whether the core of the tree had been devoured. If the sound is sufficiently hollow, the tree's fate is sealed. It is brought down with a few blows of the axe and then divided into two pieces about 1.30 m long which are peeled. Some trunks can be hollowed out to a height of about four metres. In the hollow there are the passages which are created by the termites from a mixture of saliva and sawdust. They can be easily removed by knocking on the trunk or boring out the hollow with a tube.

We left the wooden pipes stripped of their bark lying there, intending to collect them on the way back and take them back to the car. I doubted if we would ever find them again because our search led us for quite considerable distances all over the bush.

Even for people who have grown up in this climate cutting down trees is a tiring business. Moreover, David is already in his late sixties. Thus, it was not surprising that after a while he handed me the axe and told me to try my luck. As I had chopped lots of firewood that winter, I was in excellent shape. David agreed and that is why he 'allowed me' to chop down all the next trees, cut them into pieces, and peel them.

My promotion from observer to apprentice started to become

The yield of didgeridoos following
an afternoon in the bush.
(Photograph Bob Gosford)

quite a tiring business. I could imagine why it had taken so long to discover the north of Australia. In order to do any physical labour there, you need an enormous amount of strength and stamina. Under normal circumstances, the Yolngu would do this work early in the morning or late in the afternoon. The Yolngu find it incomprehensible that people tire themselves out in the blistering sun, even if there is no other way, as in the case of our expedition. This is not a matter of laziness, but of experience of the exhausting climate.

Obviously, on our way back, David easily found all the wooden pipes we had harvested . With an assurance bordering on the improbable, he went straight to the place where they were piled up, without looking round even once. I could not even have found my way back to the car, even though I was quite proud of my orienteering skills. When I asked him how he managed to find the way, he gave me the simple answer: 'You know, I can still read the country'. What else? Going into the bush with the Yolngu is a very special experience. I felt exceptionally safe. We arrived back at the car laden with trunks. The others had also found enough wooden pipes and there was nothing to stop the didgeridoo production for the time being.

We drove to a few other places to find bark for painting the pipes. David is also a master of this art. The trunks which we found were exactly right in terms of size, but when we tested the bark we found that because of a lack of water (that year the rainy season had been very late coming) the stringy bark was not yet sufficiently flexible to be easily separated from the trunk.

Didgeridoos are not the only craft products made in Wugularr. For some time the local artists have tried to set up an organization enabling them to put on joint exhibitions. Apart from didgeridoos they also make clapsticks, boomerangs, string bags woven from palm fibre and painted sculptures representing Mimi spirits (mythological figures from the Dreamtime) or animals.

We got home that evening very tired and disgustingly filthy. The wooden pipes were carelessly thrown onto the ground in front of the verandah. We quickly got changed because I still had to be introduced at the Club. The Club is located on a site surrounded by steel wire where a maximum of six cans of beer (approximately 2 litres per person) are sold from four o' clock in the afternoon on weekdays. The cans are opened at the counter so that it is not possible to sell them on. Outside the Club, alcohol is prohibited in the community. In this way it is hoped that the consumption of alcohol can be controlled to some extent. The Yolngu do all they can to support this. They launched a home-made campaign which was supported by many musicians with the slogan: 'Beat the Grog!'. White Australian society has a cliched view of Aborigines being eternal drunks with nothing better to do than convert their dole money into alcohol.

But the fact that alcoholism isn't quite so visible amongst the whites does not mean it does not exist there. For example, in the Northern Territory, distances are measured in the number of cans of beer which can be drunk in a drive from A to B. Andrew McMillan described this as follows in his book 'Strict Rules': 'Darwin to Katherine? Oh, that's a carton. Katherine to Barunga, three green cans should get you there.' The consumption of alcohol in the Territory is twice as high as in the other States.

In order to deal with the alcohol problem, a number of Yolngu tribes have set up a self-help group: the so called out-stations. Out-stations are communities where alcohol is strictly prohibited. They are so remote that a drunk will either be sober by the time he arrives, or the road is too long and difficult to bother going to find the alcohol in the first place. Increasingly the people in the out-stations are once again living in accordance with traditional customs. It is noticeable that this has a great influence on the psychological health of the people. A return to their ancient knowledge of medicine and a balanced diet ('bush tucker', i.e., food from the bush is once again on the menu), have clearly led to positive results. Diseases such as diabetes and blindness, as well as high infant mortality, which were so commonplace amongst the Aborigines that the cases were out of all proportion, have noticeably declined.

I was now in the Club. I had thought that Wugularr was a 'dry colony', and now this. In order to limit consumption, the beer is obviously much more expensive than in the bottle shop. Often there is not enough money for a daily small dose of oblivion in the Club. Enmeshed in the rules of tradition which meant that David had to share with his 'mob', he asked me again and again to lend money to all sorts of people so that they could buy a few cans and David would not have to feel ashamed. I did lend them money, although I felt inwardly opposed to this. Alcohol was just about the last way in which I wanted to show my gratitude for their hospitality. But at the same time I asked myself: 'Who do you think you are, trying to lay down the law for these people within their own rules of the game?' However, this did not take away my feeling of unease.

Making the excuse that I wanted to work on my notes, I finally got out. A little while later David appeared on the verandah and we made a pot of tea. When I asked whether he came from this district, he started to tell me something about his career. I could not understand his words very easily, and so I taped what he said, much to David's own pleasure. He greatly enjoyed hearing the recording afterwards.

The next day David and Tom started work on the wooden pipes we had brought back. David indicated the length at which I should saw them. He had made long, hollow chisels from the iron used in reinforcing concrete. He used these to sand out the termite passages in the trunks. This was very easy because the walls of the passages are very porous and they actually crumble when you push or tap them with the chisel. Finally, only the hard layers of wood which had not been devoured by the termites remained. These had to be carefully scraped out with the long chisels. The end of the didgeridoo was sanded out with a long screwdriver (in the absence of a wood chisel) to a depth of 30 or 40 cm in a funnel shape, so that the wall is relatively thin there. If the termites have done their work well, i.e., if the wall is not too thick along the entire length, the didge is merely polished on the outside with a sander.

If the internal hollow has a sufficiently large diameter but the wall is still too thick, the remaining wood is removed on the outside with an axe so that the tube tapers towards the end. The mouthpiece is treated with particular care. The end is polished very carefully with the sander. The best mouthpiece is one which does not need beeswax before it can be played. Then the didgeridoo is finished.

Dotpaintings and Copyright

The detailed painting often found nowadays on didgeridoos in galleries and souvenir shops is above all a result of the tourist industry. Perhaps it is time that we let go of the standard view of Aborigines as noble savages who lead a nomadic existence in the bush, with a didgeridoo in one hand and a boomerang in the other. In the rich cultural life of the Yolngu, didgeridoos play only a modest role. During my investigations I was struck by the fact that in many detailed books on Aboriginal art there was little or no mention at all of didgeridoos.

Like our own musical instruments, didgeridoos are used on secular as well as religious occasions. They are painted only for very special events; ordinary 'everyday' didges often have no decoration at all. The way in which didgeridoos are painted is similar to the way in which Aborigines paint their bodies for festivals and ceremonies. The motifs they use have a mythological origin and are often subject to religious taboos, so that they may only be watched by the initiated. For this reason the painted decorations are washed off immediately after the ceremony, and a didgeridoo may even be destroyed. Obviously, there were also didgeridoos in the past which were permanently painted, but this was much less common than it is now. In many cases the paintings have a totemic significance. In this case the motif is closely related to the artist's personal Dreaming. It may be displayed in public because the true history related to it is known only to the owner of the Dreaming concerned anyway. When I asked David what the figures on his didgeridoo represented, he answered only that this was a 'water beetle' – Dreaming. He would not say anything more,

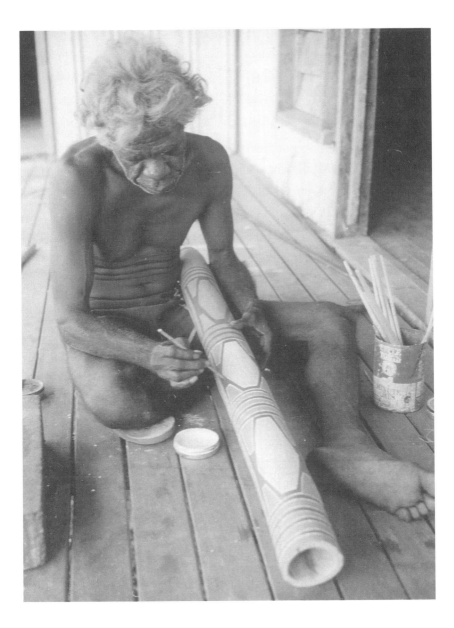

David painting a rarrk motif.

that much was clear from the tone of voice which he used. When I went to Australia for the first time in 1986 there were hardly any didgeridoos for sale in the shops selling Aborigine arts and crafts. The fact that since that time there has been a huge increase in these instruments is because of the popularity they have gained in the last few years, by no means least, because it has been increasingly used in pop music. (see Part 2) As didgeridoos are not produced only in the Northern Territory anymore, though this was where they originally came from, the ways in which they are decorated also vary considerably.

David's style is similar to that of the 'bark paintings' which are very common in Arnhemland. In comparison with other styles, bark paintings are characterized by the use of many human and animal figures. Events or figures from the Dreamtime (the time when everything was created) are represented, or totemic figures of the artist himself.

In simple terms, the Yolngu assume that the ancient Forefathers, the heroes from the Dreamtime, created the world and everything in it by singing, dancing and giving names. To do so they often assumed a human figure first, and then, after the creation, they changed into animals, trees or geographical formations which still exist and which therefore have an important place in spiritual life. The Yolngu's style of painting was influenced by contacts with the outside world. For centuries the 'Macassans' came to the north coast at regular times to find sea cucumbers. These contacts, which were usually peaceful, left their traces on the Yolngu culture.

It is possible to determine the age of this tradition of painting from the many rock paintings, some of which are 20 to 30,000 years old. The so-called X-ray style can already be identified in these paintings. The 'X-ray style' refers to a way of representing animals so that their organs and skeletal structure are shown on their bodies with remarkable anatomical precision.

A constantly recurring element which determines the style of the bark paintings is the shading using very thin white and coloured lines which cross over and are called 'rarrk'. To make the colours only earth pigments are used, found by the artist himself in the surrounding area or traded with someone else.

The colours are called ochres. There are yellow ochres and red ochres. White is made using a white clay, and black using charcoal or soot. These colours are not mixed to produce new colours. The dyes are ground on a rough stone. The piece of pigment is rubbed on the stone until there is an adequate amount of powder. The powder is then mixed with water and a binding agent. In the past, the yolk of an egg was used for this, or sometimes the milky sap of white orchids or the resin of the eucalyptus tree. Nowadays the artists use wood glue thinned with water. The paint is mixed on the stone and used straight from the stone. There is a separate stone for each colour which is used only for that colour.

David always used yellow as the basic colour for his didgeridoos. On top of this he painted a geometric pattern in red outlined in white, and then filled it in with the shading described above. In addition to 'modern' brushes, he used a sort of drawing brush for the 'rarrk' and for the outlines. The hairs of this brush are 4 to 5 cm long and consist of human hair or the fibrous parts of a special sort of reed. The stems of the plants are carefully beaten with a piece of wood. This produces a mushy substance and the long, thin fibres can be fished out one by one. Five or six of these fibres are enough for a drawing brush. The fibres are tied onto a pointed stick with thread, and are then cut off all at the same length.

David painted line after line with infinite patience; I only became aware of the precision with which he did this when I tried to do it myself. The dots were painted with a cotton bud or the stem of a plant.

The style which has become best known is that of the dot-paintings. This style is nowadays also used on didgeridoos, though it originally came from central Australia. The painters' movement of the Aborigines started with these dot paintings in 1971. The school building of the community of Papunya (Central Australia) was to be painted by the children. As it was rather a lot for them to do on their own, they were helped by a few older Anangu, which is the name of the people in that region. These men revealed an astonishing sense of form and colour. When the school project had been completed, the teacher, Geoffrey Bardon, encouraged them to try their skill with acrylic paint on linen.

Drawing brush made of plant fibre.

Of course it was an ancient tradition, going back to the sacred sand paintings which were made on smoothed areas of sand for ritual purposes. Insofar as a comparison is appropriate, the tension evoked in these sand paintings by the perfect design and meticulous geometric execution is comparable to the best examples of traditional Japanese gardens.

Stones, feathers, plants and different sands with varying colours were used. Because of the transient nature of these works of art, they were not seen by white men for a long time, particularly as only initiates were admitted to most ceremonies. Sand mosaics were made by men as well as women. The tradition was now masterfully recorded by the Anangu, using acrylic paints on linen. The patterns and figures were painted on the linen in thousands of colourful dots.

One could say that thousands of years before the Impressionists were working in France, these people had already discovered Pointillism. These paintings are also to some extent subject to religious taboos. That is why there was some disagreement among the Anangu about the question of what could and what could not be shown to the public.

Once they were discovered by white art dealers, the dot paintings started a stormy career, although the sale – and therefore most of the profits – unfortunately remained in the hands of the whites. The decorative value of the paintings was soon discovered by industry. The motifs were printed on materials and T-shirts – though the artists were never paid for their copyright!

Nowadays, there is an organization which supports artists with regard to these and similar problems. Chris McGuigan of the AAMA (Aboriginal Arts Management Association) told me about a case in which a carpet factory had copied, dot by dot, a painting from a museum catalogue although this painting had been especially made for this museum and had a special ritual significance.

For the artists it was a great shock to find that their sacred motifs would literally be walked all over. What would devout Christians think if carpeting appeared on the market with representations of the Crucifixion?

Let's return to the didgeridoo. A third method of decoration is applied which involves burning motifs into the wood with glowing steel wire. Again there are geometric patterns and representations of heroes from the Dreamtime.

It took David three days to paint a didgeridoo, obviously interrupted at regular intervals by endless breaks during which he kept up a busy social life. Dealers came to Wugulaar with clockwork regularity to buy didgeridoos. Even top figures such as David get remarkably little money for their work, when you compare it with the money earned by a white craftsman.

The saddest didge trading which I came across was the exchange of a didgeridoo for beer. In the morning the driver of a small truck which was going to Katherine to pick up components for tools was given two beautiful didgeridoos. In Katherine he sold them to a local dealer, but on his way back he exchanged the proceeds for two crates of beer. Just outside the alcohol boundary we discovered the didgeridoo salesman who had made his fortune, obviously together with his 'mob' who had heard all about the transaction. The beer was unloaded and it was a huge success: the drunken, stumbling partygoers caused havoc in the community until late that night. The consequences of this sort of behaviour are violence and poverty, just as they are in our own community. It certainly did not make me feel very good. It was not that I was physically threatened myself, but all the same, the mood was rather uncomfortable.

In fact, my presence in Wugulaar was certainly not accepted everywhere just like that. Several times I was asked to justify myself by young Yolngu. What did I think I was doing there? Was I one of those people who wanted to profit from the last bit of surviving Yolngu culture? What good was it to them that a few people in Europe could play the didgeridoo a little; it certainly wouldn't improve their own situation. My response that the different cultures should be able to come together with some mutual respect, was met with a tired smile. They had their own experiences of this so-called mutual respect.

Another important experience I had related to sharing. Every Yolngu is obliged to share everything he has with his mob.

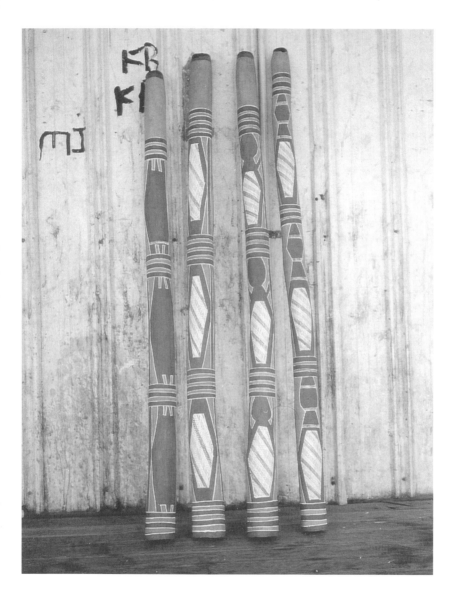

**Four of Tom Kelly's didgeridoos
which had already been sold.**

Because of a complicated family structure, almost everyone is related to everyone else, even if it is only because they have the same 'skin name'.

This system obliges the Yolngu to share: anyone who has, shares. In his turn, anyone who gives can count on profiting from this system himself in time of need. This applies to everything, even to lending vehicles; the possible 'death' of the vehicle is simply accepted. Anyone who tries to make a career along western lines does not usually enjoy his increased prosperity for very long because the whole mob hangs around his neck straightaway. He is obliged to feed them all – 'strict rules!'.

Nowadays, this phenomenon is one of the causes of poverty. It is no mean feat to maintain a balance between the two cultures when one wants to get ahead by working hard at the same time. For whites who are not really familiar with the traditional backgrounds, this is quite incomprehensible. David taught me to get used to filling our fridge every morning. During the course of the day he would share out the contents amongst the mob who came to visit more and more often. After a while I didn't care any more; I just kept stocking up the supplies and David would share them out again. Gratitude did not come into it. Once you are in the system, it is taken for granted that you turn up whenever you need anything.

A white infant teacher told me once that from a certain age children are only given a certain amount of food by their mothers. They have to find the rest from the clan. Meanwhile, the production of a number of didgeridoos was completed. This meant that I had spent quite a while in Wugularr and that my stay with David was coming to an end. Living with these people had been a curious and conflicting experience. Many questions remained unanswered, though these were related less to the subject of didgeridoos than to general matters.

Was it really an illusion that the Yolngu culture and the western culture could co-exist equally or even side by side?

My departure was as uneventful as my arrival had been. If I ever go back I am sure there will be a place for me by the verandah, and a fridge to fill.

Part Two

Didgeridoo Goes Rock

The Rise of 'Black Music'

The best known names in the Australian pop world are AC/DC, INXS and Midnight Oil. The obvious similarity between these groups is the white colour of the skin of their members. Black musicians have succeeded in being included in the mainstream only recently. But it is still much more difficult for them than it is for comparable white artists. It is worth studying the field of 'black music' more closely, because this is where some of the impulses have come from, and these certainly had an effect on 'white' music.

The didgeridoo owes its current popularity for a large part to the fact that Koori musicians have consistently used it in their version of pop music. The first anthropologists who came across these instruments did not really take it seriously. In many musical lexicons the didgeridoo is not even mentioned under the heading 'Australian instruments'. The first thorough research was carried out in the early 1960s by Trevor A. Jones (The Didgeridoo of the Australian Aborigine) and Alice M. Moyle (Bara and Mamariga songs on Groote Island).

With the growing efforts to attain the right of self-determination, a black pop music culture developed in the 1960s. Bands were founded which played mainly ballads in the tradition of Country & Western, Country Gospel and Hillbilly. Some of the great examples included Elvis Presley and Charley Pride, and this music is still popular. Usually the bands performed only for black audiences.

The CASM (Centre for Aboriginal Studies in Music) was founded in the early 1970s as an independent department of the University of Adelaide with the main aim of giving young Koori musicians an opportunity for further training. Initially, only young Koori musicians were trained there and in addition the traditional music was studied and recorded. Obviously these musicians did not escape the cultural influences of life in the modern city. The first rock bands were soon formed from the students of the CASM. These bands obviously used the traditional instruments and they tried to integrate their own characteristic music. The performance of Bob Marley, a black superstar, in Adelaide in 1979, was of decisive importance with regard to the musical self-confidence of black musicians. His message: 'All blacks are brothers!' gave many people the strength to perform their music in the outside world despite all the opposition. Even when the bands played reggae it was 'Aboriginal Reggae'.

The groups 'No Fixed Address' and 'Us Mob', developed from this movement. No Fixed Address is particularly reggae oriented. The characteristic feature of their style is the combination of Country & Western influences with the use of traditional instruments, with which they succeed in painting entire musical landscapes. It does not really appeal to reggae purists at all.

By contrast, Us Mob has focused more on the heavy metal rock. Heavy metal is usually associated with political provocation. This seems to be rather a contradiction in terms for a Koori band; but when I asked them about it, the members of the band told me that their greatest musical influence was Jimi Hendrix and that their music was certainly intended to be hard and aggressive because of the message they wished to spread.

In any case, both bands constantly focus attention in their lyrics on Koori interests.

'They promise us this, and they promise us that. But all we ever get is a stab in the back. They tell us what to do and they push us around, And then they have the gall to push us around. (Chorus) When are they going to learn, when will they stop ? When are they going to learn to stop this genocide?'. (From 'Genocide', by Peter Butler and Wally McArthur).

The possibilities for development for these groups in the white music industry were obviously very limited. Although their audiences had long since changed – and half of the audience was now white – the existence of these bands was obstinately denied by the 'musical establishment'. Concerts were regularly cancelled at short notice, and it proved impossible to conclude good recording contracts. When Sade was on tour in Australia a few years ago, she wanted a Koori support group. The organisers simply told her that there were no Koori bands.

'I think our biggest feeling when we are on stage is seeing mixed people together. Like with half the crowd white and half the crowd black, getting along together with no trouble. Most of the blackfellas who come to see us feel really proud. We're just trying to get respected.' B. Willoughby, NFA.

'What we are basically on about is to show the gubbahs that we are not a bunch of drunks, we are talented and we are proud to prove it.' P. Butler, Us Mob.

Some groups gave up trying to compete with the mainstream. Or at least changed their tactics and performed in their own environment and then only occasionally. The members of these groups usually earn their living with totally different work. A distinction should also be made between the 'urban bands' and the 'outback bands'. The members of these latter groups are often more closely tied to a more traditional way of life which provides them with a social context, although this cultural link with the ancient traditions regularly makes life difficult for musicians when the traditional obligations do not correspond with the tour schedule. The Warumpi Band is a typical example of this sort of group. It comes from the red heart of Australia. The Warumpis come from Papunya. They are locally based and have had to deal with all the difficulties which normally confront Anangu bands. Their first album, 'Big Name, No Blankets', emphatically expresses their often extremely precarious financial situation. In 1983, they brought out the first rock single in the Anangu language with 'Jailangu Pakarnu' (Released from Jail). It was produced by CAAMA (Central Australian Aboriginal Media Association) in Alice Springs. This media organization developed in 1980 from a small radio station which started up with modest broadcasts lasting half an hour in the various languages of central Australia. Following the radio station, a television station and recording studio were also set up. CAAMA is completely run by the Koori. Their aim is to protect and maintain the cultural identity of the original population with the help of the modern media. Even in the most remote communities in the bush the population can listen to broadcasts in their own language about subjects such as health, education, taxation and their own traditional wealth of stories. CAAMA broadcasts radio programmes in the seven most important languages. It produces its own television films, and in the sound studio groups can make professional recordings at a fair price.

CAAMA has already produced more than 40 of its own albums and that does not include the countless recordings which have been broadcast on the radio but no record has yet been made.

CAAMA can also respond quickly and appropriately to the interests of the Koori.

For example, Mark Manolis, the sound technician, told me that twice an album has had to be withdrawn because the members of the band concerned had died.

In fact, death is traditionally surrounded with strong taboos. When someone dies his name may not be mentioned for a long time and in some circumstances, never; for a period his artistic works may not be distributed. If reference has to be made to him or her, he/she is referred to as 'Kumanjayi': 'The one without a name'. The Elders decide when and whether the taboo can be lifted.

No 'normal' recording company would want to or even be able to accept these rules.

If living persons happen to have the same name as someone who has died they often assume another name. For this reason the singer and leader of the band Yothu Yindi, Bakamana Yunipingu is now called Mandawuy Yunipingu.

Mark Manolis mentioned another special phenomenon, viz. that even the oldest members of the clan were involved in the performances of the bands. They went to most of the concerts – even the loudest rock concerts. Their pride and fascination in seeing their own people on the stage was greater than any problems they might have had with decibels.

Meanwhile, black musicians are no longer alone in their fight for recognition. They are supported in their struggle by white colleagues who are in turn inspired by Koori music.

To begin with, there is the Australian band 'Midnight Oil', known simply as 'The Oils' in Australia. They are often thought of one of the rock bands with the strongest political views and have been compared with the Irish band U2 in terms of their commitment. It certainly seems that they do not shun any of the controversial issues: the environment, nuclear energy, unemployment, corruption, racism – all these are subjects for their songs. But the most remarkable thing is that their commitment is not limited to writing lyrics. A considerable portion of their income goes into social and political projects.

The term 'solid' is often used with reference to this band, and it certainly seems justified. The slogan 'sex, drugs 'n rock and roll' does not really apply, though this certainly does not mean that they don't put on a good show or that they are rather tame. Midnight Oil has supported the careers of many colleagues, both white and black. On the Australian rock scene, Midnight Oil is omnipresent. During the mid-1980s the band focused its attention on the Koori population of Australia and their struggle for the right of self-determination.

As they like to put into practice what they sing about, they organized a tour in 1986 which took the group to the most remote Yolngu communities in the Northern Territory; this was called the 'Blackfella/Whitefella tour'. They were supported by the Warumpi Band. For four weeks bands travelled through the desert and the tropical north in land rovers and small charter planes. A band which is used to performing for crowds of tens of thousands of people were playing for at most a few hundred Yolngu, who had never seen anything like it.

The experiences of this trip inspired Midnight Oil to produce their album 'Diesel and Dust', which came out in 1987.

Many Australian musicians work in close collaboration with each other. Thus, it is not surprising that Charly McMahon was appointed as a scout and leader for the Blackfella/Whitefella tour. Because of his years of experience in the outback he was the perfect man to ensure that everything went as smoothly as possible in the bush. He performed similar work for the German film-maker, Wim Wenders, when he came to Australia to make parts of his film 'Till the End of the Earth'. In answer to the question what Charly McMahon knows about music – or, in particular, about didgeridoos – we can simply say that he is one of the few musicians who has become famous solely as a didgeridoo player.

For a large part of his youth Charly lived in the bush. He came into contact with didgeridoos at a young age. It is said that he sometimes stayed out in the bush for days on end.

When his family moved to Sydney, Charly took up a dangerous hobby: he started to play around with rockets. He lost his right hand in an explosion. Because of this handicap he was more or less forced to take up a university career. He took degrees in economics and sociology – one after the other – but blood is thicker than water and the bush always enticed him back. In the end, Charly was more of a practical than a theoretical man. He started to work with Aborigines in Kintore. He drilled for water, supervised the construction of landing strips and co-ordinated the building of houses.

Charly gave his first performance with an electronically amplified didgeridoo in 1978 with Midnight Oil, whom he had met by chance at one of their performances. They spontaneously invited him to accompany them. Together with the synthesizer performer, Peter Carolan, he started the 'Gondwanaland Project'. This was a project because neither of them was sure if their music would be a commercial success. The name Gondwanaland refered the southern subcontinent going back to a period before the various continents had moved away from each other and spread out over the surface of the earth into the places where they are now. Gondwanaland toured from 1981, and in 1985 the members of the group, with the addition of the percussionist Eddie Duquemin, became full-time musicians. Carried by the rhythmic sound of the didgeridoo, Gondwanaland developed a completely unique style. The combination of the didgeridoo and the synthesizer formed a bridge across thousands of years of musical history. The undulating sounds created in this way not only formed the basis of meditative music, but were also applied in a way which provoked an amazing audience response.

Charly McMahon never betrayed his links with the spiritual world of the Koori. He does not call the works which he played with Gondwanaland 'songs', but 'stories'.

He uses ten different didgeridoos, each in a different key. The instrument which Charly calls a 'didgeribone' is rather different: a cross between a trombone and a didgeridoo. Two wooden tubes placed one inside the other can be moved to and fro while the instrument is played, as in the case of a trombone, so that different notes are produced. Charly McMahon also works with film. He made a documentary about David Blanasi. The sound of his didgeridoo can be heard in numerous feature films as background music, e.g., in 'Till the End of the World' and 'Mad Max – Beyond the Thunderdome'. He even made the didgeridoo a 'civilized' instrument by performing with the London Philharmonic Orchestra.

One of the most remarkable careers in the Australian music world is that of the group, 'Yothu Yindi'. The members of the band originate from the northeast of Arnhemland, a part of Australia which only came into contact with white culture late in the day because of its inaccessible position, and which is still fairly isolated even now. The name of the group means something like 'Mother and Child', as well as 'Child of the Earth'. More than any other rock group, they have succeeded in combining their musical tradition with rock. They sing partly in English and partly in Gumatj, a Yolngu language. Occasionally they play purely traditional pieces, exclusively with clapsticks, didgeridoo and song. The albums 'Homeland Movement' and 'Tribal Voice' are good examples of such musical combinations.

The didgeridoo player Milkayngu Mununggurr, is one of the stylistic supports of the group. Again and again he successfully adapts his style to the requirements of western music; moreover, his tempo is fairly high ! In fact, he does not refer to his instrument as a didgeridoo, but calls it a yidaki – the Yolngu word for didgeridoo.

Usually, the term yidaki refers to an instrument which is slightly shorter than the average didgeridoo and which is played with a much faster tempo.

The explanation for Yothu Yindi's success is not only the general popularity of ethno rock. The lyrics are too obviously political for this. Perhaps it is due to the group's dynamic strength which adds power to the message from a world which is foreign to us. The musicians do not conceal their origins in any way. They perform with painted bodies and throw themselves into a wild performance, so that their music is filled with extraordinary expression.

Since it was founded in 1986, the group has made several tours and have more or less travelled round the world. In North America they performed as special guests, supporting Midnight Oil (the Oils again!), on their tour 'Diesel and Dust to Big Mountain, Rights for Indigenous People'. This tour brought them into contact with the North American Indians. Together with Tracy Chapman, they performed in New Zealand, and they have also visited several places in Europe.

But on all these trips the group always retained and emphasized its deep links with its own country.

The leader of the group, Mundawuy Yunupingu, is an unusual figure in many respects. He was one of the first Yolngu from Arnhemland to get an academic degree. He became head of the Yittakala Community School and introduced a curriculum which provided the pupils with elements of both cultures, the European and the Yolngu culture. In 1993, he was given the title of Australian of the Year on Australia Day; this was the same man who had been refused entrance to a restaurant in

Melbourne only a year earlier because his skin was the wrong colour.

'Building Bridges' is the name of a musical project involving both black and white bands, and it has already produced its first record. Their aim is to work for a future in which all Australians will have the same rights. Meanwhile, a magazine has also been started: '12 to 15'. This is not so much focusing on music as its main topic, but is consciously aimed at the deprived Aborigine youth.

At the 'Survival Festival' in Sydney I met Jim George who was permanently employed on the Building Bridges project. Despite all the successes, mainly of Yothu Yindi, he painted a rather bleak picture of the state of affairs in the Australian music business, at least as regards the opportunities for the development of black musicians at that time. Though he agreed that Yothu Yindi's mega hit, 'Treaty', was the right song for the moment, and that the group was brilliant with its exotic performances, it was still very much an exception. Other excellent Koori musicians were still small time, just as in the past, and somewhere Yothu Yindi's political message, meaningful though it was, had been lost on the dance floor. Australian youngsters were simply having a wild time in discos with this new sound, complete with a token Koori from down the road.

According to Jim, a good indication of the success of musicians was the amount of money they had in their pockets. This was clearly still lacking. By way of example he mentioned Kev Carmody, a very professional songwriter who had already produced two albums. Half of his performances consisted of benefit gigs for almost exclusively black audiences. He could only really earn anything at the large festivals. It sometimes happened that he and his colleague, Rory Mcleod, went home from tour with 150 dollars in their pockets, while the roadies had earned 450 dollars. It is entirely due to the ignorance of Australian recording companies that many Koori musicians had to go to America or Europe to start their careers there. In fact, the same applies to white musicians. It is only when they have made their name and fame somewhere outside Australia that they are recognized in their own country.

In any case, the success of Yothu Yindi will eventually open a few doors and at least make it easier for some other musicians to join the mainstream.

I telephoned Peter Garrett of Midnight Oil, and though this did not result in the interview I had hoped for (after all, I'm not writing for *Rolling Stone*), it did lead to a good contact with Denise Brewster who works for the Office, which is where all the Oil's activities are co-ordinated. When she is not working for the Office, she is manager of the Sunrize Band from Meningrida in the Northern Territory.

The first time I met the band was just before a performance in Darwin where they were giving an introductory concert for a tour through the whole of Australia. A typically Australian gig takes place in a bar or club, and as space is always limited in these places, there is often a lot of overcrowding. The Yolngu are amply represented in the population of Darwin so that when a black band performs the Yolngu are always present. As a European, it was a strange experience for me to be one of the no more than 15 white concertgoers there. The fact that alcohol was served unfortunately meant that I became the target of out-and-out physical provocation. It was quite difficult to make sure that the situation did not get out of hand. It was a strange feeling to suddenly belong to a minority group.

There are always two different possible ways of reacting, and as I obstinately opted for the peaceful route, the situation gradually became more relaxed and finally I had the pleasure of experiencing the very special sensation of this sort of concert.

The Sunrize Band is a rock band entirely loyal to the motto, 'Sing Loud, Play Strong', without any loss of musical quality. The singer and lead guitarist gave free rein to his admiration for Jimi Hendrix. To the delight of his audience he was able to perform all the tricks which his great example managed to do on the E string. Apart from this, the use of the didgeridoo and the clapsticks also determine the sound of this band. Their lyrics, like those of many others, are about the daily life of the

Yolngu. 'Land Rights' is one of the titles which spring to mind in this respect.

The didgeridoo player Horace Waluwala was visiting his family at the same time that I was in Wugularr where we got to know each other. I then accompanied the Sunrize band at a number of their gigs. It started with the exhausting tour of the smaller clubs, but fortunately they also had an opportunity to take part in 'Survival '93'.

This festival was a sort of counter-festival to Australia Day, the national holiday of Australia. On that day in 1788, the 'First Fleet' landed in Botany Bay with colonists and convicts. Obviously this is not particularly a day to celebrate for the Koori. They call it 'Invasion Day'. 'Survival '93' is a concert which takes place at the entrance to the above-mentioned bay. Only Koori groups take part. There is no entrance fee, just one rule which every visitor must observe: 'No grog!' (no alcohol). The range of performers comprises artists such as the songwriter, Kev Carmody, the 'Bangarara Dance Theatre', big bands like 'Djaambi', playing rhythm and blues, and the 'rockers', the 'Warumpi Band', 'Sunrize' and 'Mixed Relations'. It was striking that absolutely all of the rock groups used a didgeridoo, even the groups from the south.

There was an easy relaxed atmosphere, perhaps because whole families had come together. In fact, half of the audience was white. This festival is a true meeting place of different cultures. The organizers counted 20,000 visitors, just as many as the 'Big Day Out' concert, which is the more or less 'official' rock concert announced in the media with a great furore.

As we read in the newspaper the next day, that event was by no means as peaceful as the 'Survival '93' – the 'Festival of the Savages'.

The first time I met a white didgeridoo player was by pure chance in a cafe. He came in with a rucksack on his back and a didgeridoo under his arm. Of course I said hello. He called himself Johnny Didge and originally came from the Gippslands, south east of Melbourne. In the 1960s he had organized screenings of documentary films about Aborigines.

**The Sunrize Band at the
Survival '93 festival.**

This work first brought him into contact with the instrument. For a time he worked in Darwin, where he took the opportunity to find out more about didgeridoos. From time to time he went to Melbourne to earn some money busking – i.e., performing as a street musician. In Australia, this is a popular 'sport': people like to busk and like to see buskers. Johnny was quite typical of many of the musicians I met, though he has a very individual style: he rapidly alternates the trombone sound and then plays with a fluttering tongue. I have never heard anything remotely like this in the traditional ways of playing. Johnny sells an interesting cassette, 'Spirit of Place', which he produced himself and on which he can be heard with a singer who uses the technique of singing harmonics.

Andrew Langford is another white didgeridoo musician. I also met him 'by chance' in Alice Springs. I saw a small photograph on which I recognized David Blanaisi with a white man in a gallery for Aboriginal arts and crafts (there are about a thousand of these in Alice). As I was curious, I asked the owner of the gallery who the other man in the photograph was. I told her that I knew David very well. The lady picked up the telephone straightaway and Andrew came into the shop a little later.

Andrew has mastered an astonishing range of the most diverse sounds, all of which which he manages to produce with his didgeridoo quite effortlessly. His style can best be characterized by the term 'percussive': the strong rhythms are characteristic. When Andrew plays, you get the feeling that he is creating the sound deep in his stomach. He told me that he works mainly from the diaphragm. He is able to blow two trombone notes with different pitches. He has produced a cassette in the CAAMMA studios, together with Ted Egan, a singer of country ballads. Half of this consists of didgeridoo music and half of ballads.

Increasingly Andrew has also worked with classical musicians, (string players, wind players, guitarists). He had plans to produce an album based on this co-operation.

In Sydney, I visited the musician, Alan Dargin. His musical emphasis is also on the didgeridoo. He was taught to play the instrument by his grandfather when he was only five years old. As a Yolngu, he was obviously familiar with many traditional rhythms, but there were a number which he never played in public because they are intended for very special ceremonies. Alan has been travelling around the world with his didgeridoo for years and has performed in Europe, Japan and the United States. On his album, 'Bloodwood', he plays with the multi-instrumentalist, Michael Atherton, who has made his name with numerous film compositions. It is particularly worth listening to a recording on which Alan is playing in the street and uses the didgeridoo to relate the story of a hitchhiker, 'Hitchhikers nightmare', to an excited audience. On the same cassette he can be heard on a didgeridoo made of bloodwood, which is more than 100 years old, and which was the inspiration for the name of the album.

When Alan played with the Irish group, 'Reconciliation', this led to a very special cultural encounter. This group plays a bronze Irish horn, the 'dord'. The oldest instruments of this kind to be dug up in Ireland are about 3,000 years old. It was only a few years ago that the musician, Rolf Harris, solved the mystery of how these horns should be played: in the same way as a didgeridoo! The Irishman, Simon O'Dwyer, plays faithful imitations of this ancient instrument. His colleagues are not always convinced by his use of the instrument in Irish folk music; so the first album on which the dord and the didgeridoo could be heard together was entitled: 'Two stories in One: (Natural Symphonies)'. Alan also occasionally goes 'busking' – for him it's all part of it.

However, the didgeridoo has not only been introduced in rock and pop music. The Australian composer, Moya Henderson, used the instrument in her work 'Sacred Site'. This piece forges a symbolic link with the Aborigine culture. It is written for organ and tape recorder.

The premier of the work took place in the Sydney Opera House. This world-famous opera building is built on a spot which is considered sacred by the Koori.

The co-operation between George Winunguj (from Goulborn Island) and the Melbourne composer, George Dreyfus, who originates from Germany, reached a peak in a recording with the 'Adelaide Wind Quintet'. On the album, 'Sextet for Didgeridoo and Wind Instruments', Dreyfus proved that the didgeridoo is also quite at home in the world of classically-oriented music. During the quintet's world tour in 1973, George Winunguj's performance was the high point of every concert. Once more he proved that in the hands of a virtuoso the didgeridoo is certainly more than a windpipe which produces undifferentiated noises.

In this detailed description of parts of the Australian music world, I have endeavoured to give a picture of the way in which the didgeridoo is finding its way into the mainstream as a musical instrument with a 'message'. For the time being, it is a matter of waiting to see to what extent this is just one of the vagaries of fashion, or whether the didgeridoo will really be taken seriously as a musical instrument.

**Mandawuy Yunupingu and members of the ten man band,
Yothu Yindi, during their performance in Munich in 1993.**

Rock 'n Roll with
the Heroes of the Dreamtime

Despite all my unsuccessful efforts to arrange an interview in Australia with Mandawuy Junupingu, the lead singer of Yothu Yindi, I suddenly succeeded in arranging an interview with him while I was still working on this book. I met the band just before their concert in Munich and had the opportunity to talk to a few of its members. I had an interview with Mandawuy which lasted forty minutes. It would be a bit much to write down everything we discussed so I have edited the text of our conversation.

Dirk: Mandawuy, why do you think our culture has become so interested in the Aborigines and their culture in the last few years: in the paintings, music and spiritual values?
Mandawuy: We have something to offer white people ! Our culture was denied for 200 years, but despite everything, it has remained strong and alive. Because of the clash of the two cultures, there are gaps which we can bridge, for example, with our music. We have lived in the same spiritual tradition for thousands of years and I believe this has a value which many other people are seeking. One of the reasons why we perform with our bodies painted, is to reveal the energy which we represent. Many people are fed up with their civilization, religion, politics and all that sort of thing. We Yolngu have a definite idea of the direction we want to take. We have proved that we can learn to live in your culture, but I feel strong and proud in my own culture. It is time that you learnt something

about my civilization.

Dirk: For me you seem to be like wanderers between two worlds. Aren't you often afraid that you and your message will be snowed under by all the commercialism which goes with show business ?

Mandawuy: Yes, it's not easy. For me it is important not to be corrupted in my own culture because that happens all too easily. When problems arise in the group we try to solve them together. We do this at the 'community level'. I can go to my tribal Elders and ask them for advice about what I might be doing right and what I might be doing wrong.

The elders also have the job of keeping the band and their message together. In this way we are always in contact with our Yolngu lifestyle. Our name shows this; it stands for the two sides of life, the ordinary world and the spiritual world. The boundaries between these two areas are not clearly outlined for us but tend to merge together.

There is another thing which you should know about Yothu Yindi: our money goes back to the community. I share the money with my family and it is quite a large family! Sharing is part of our belief, our philosophy and our strength. Eventually we are planning to open our own cultural centre so that we can really support the generations to come. Everything which relates to the band comes from that single point of energy, our culture. We certainly feel that we are the 'aboriginal Australians'.

Dirk: Have you ever made contacts with other native population groups in your many tours all over the world ? Could you compare their situation with that of the original inhabitants of Australia ?

Mandawuy: In this respect we have had most contact with the Indians in North America. But I thought it was much more interesting to discover that there are still white ancient tribes in Europe! We met them in the north of Scandinavia. It was an extraordinary experience which pointed out my own short-comings to me. White natives... It was only then that I became aware of the limitations of my own way of thinking. I now realize that there could be people like us all over the world.

The situation of the Indians corresponds to ours in a number of ways. For example, in religion, the field of land rights, settling in their 'own' traditional areas, and the mining companies which are after the mineral wealth. I have had an opportunity of talking to these people on a number of occasions, to compare differences and to try and find solutions.

Dirk: We live in a world which is becoming smaller all the time and distances are getting shorter; what do you think, would it be possible to build up a network of all the ancient peoples who still live on earth?

Mandawuy: Something like that is already happening, and I would very much like to be involved. In fact, we have already started, certainly in individual areas.

Dirk: Do you think that the culture of the North American Indians is still intact to the same extent as the culture which can be found amongst the Yolngu in Australia?

Mandawuy: Yes, in my experience it was. When people come to us, the native population, they do so because they are looking for strength, they want to feel the energy that we represent.

Dirk: Before you started devoting yourself solely to music, you were actively involved in Yirrkala, setting up an educational system which was aimed at creating links between the curriculum of western white culture with that of your own culture, on an equal basis. Can you give me some idea of how this can work? Don't you find that you come up against contradictory interests?

Mandawuy: We were looking for a way of breaking through the system and fighting the authority so that we could be liberated from the patronizing approach of institutionalized racism. Nowadays, it is necessary to follow two paths at the same time if you want to survive in this world. That is simply the way it is. We would like to explain to the establishment: listen to us, our knowledge is just as important as yours! We are looking for a balance. When the whites ask, 'But how will you learn mathematics and other sciences?' I merely answer: it's all there! But we take our children into the bush instead of sitting them down in classrooms for hours on end. It's easy to imagine how our children feel in a western school: 'bloody bored'. In the bush, children learn something about nature, about our Ancestors, about the land and its boundaries. Obviously they also learn to do sums and English. It may be the case that we learn it all in our own way, but the result is the same. Every person should be allowed to decide for himself which path he should take. Forcing people to learn this or that and ignore their own culture is another form of genocide.

Dirk: Do you think that at the moment there is an exchange of views in Australian society?

Mandawuy: Oh yes, I have even had an opportunity of talking to the prime minister to tell him how I feel as a native Australian. He has a fairly straightforward view on this subject. He thinks that if it is possible for Yolngu to take part in Australian society while keeping their own cultural identity, the society would permanently change and would certainly become richer as a result. A process of reconciliation has started, and who knows, it may end with a treaty or something like that.

Dirk: Let's talk about Aborigine music. As far as I can see there are lots of bands so there's great potential, but in commercial terms there's an enormous gap between those bands and Yothu Yindi. Will the success of Yothu Yindi change this in any way?

Mandawuy: We clear the jungle – because of the unique character of our show, we have shown in just a short while what an aboriginal band can achieve. There are so many bands which have existed longer than we have, but who do even not have a recording contract yet. We are characterized by our self-consciousness and traditional reticence, at the same time as being open to new ideas. Perhaps these other bands have not had so much luck up to now. But certainly the music industry is becoming increasingly interested in Yolngu bands and prejudices are slowing being overcome. For example, I have heard that 'Mixed Relations' has just signed a recording contract. There is light at the end of the tunnel.

Dirk: As you know, my book is mainly about yidakis (didgeridoos). They are an important part of your performance. Could you tell me something more about this?

Mandawuy: If you like, you could talk to one of our yidaki

players about this, that might be more interesting.
Dirk: O.K. Mandawuy, thank you for talking to me.

Of course, the conversation I had with Makuma was very different from what I had imagined. Unlike the experienced man-of-the-world, Mandawuy, I had to forget my intellectual question-and-answer game. I was confronted with the shyness which I have often encountered in Australia as soon as the Yolngu come across a white man. It was a very short conversation, though it soon clarified the boundaries and patterns of thought.

For example, I asked why no women play the didgeridoo. He explained that women were not strong enough to breathe as powerfully as men. Moreover, women were not allowed to play the yidaki because it was a man's task. He opened his eyes wide as though I had asked a very indecent question. The only answer he gave to my questions about ceremonies was that he played the didgeridoo on these occasions.

When I asked about healing rituals I seemed to come up against a complete lack of understanding. Then I noticed that I had forgotten to turn on my microphone at the start of our interview and I decided to use this as a pretext to put an end to the conversation politely. Of course, it's not really possible to gain information in a few minutes backstage which others have taken years to collect, after spending a long time in the field. Later Mandawuy and I met once again and we talked about all sorts of things. I told him about my conversation with Makuma and he confirmed that my questions had touched too closely on certain subjects about which Mandawuy himself did not really know what he could say. All the parts of the performance of Yothu Yindi are discussed with the Elders so that everyone can be certain that no taboos are broken.

Until just before the performance we talked some more about what it was like to travel all the time; in 1992, Yothu Yindi were on the road for nine months. The members of the band gathered together, sat down and sang folk songs together. There was not a trace of stage fright.

At the point at which the group went on stage, I left the

Yothu Yindi's didgeridoo section
There is an interesting didge in front of
the player on the left.
The end consists partly of the root,
so that there is a large spherical sound funnel.

impersonal neon-lit area backstage. When I entered the concert hall where the audience sat it was as though I was entering another world. Immediately the space was filled with the pulsating energy of Yothu Yindi. There was no distance at all between the band and the audience – they understood each other straightaway.

Part 3

The Didgeridoo
as a
Therapeutic Instrument

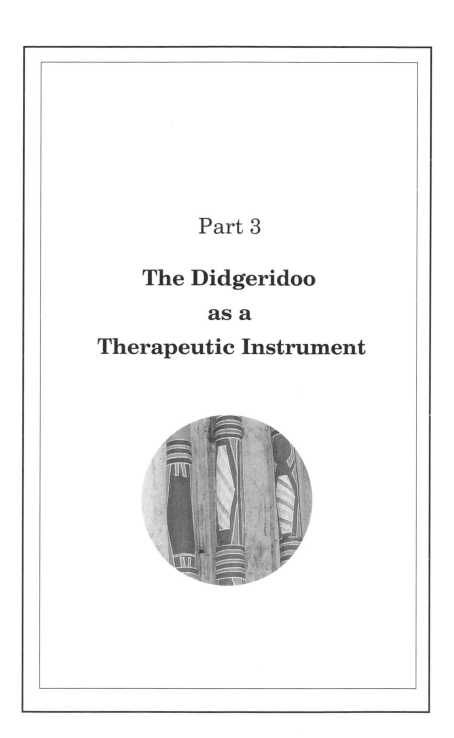

Healing with a Didgeridoo?

While I was travelling, I occasionally heard stories about 'healings' which had apparently been achieved with a didgeridoo. But as soon as I talked to the Yolngu about this their answers became curiously vague.

'Oh yes', they would say. 'There is something like that, you play on the part of the body that hurts'. But they would not or could not say more.

Obviously I also raised the subject while I was staying with David Blanasi. He also gave an evasive answer - he did not have anything special to say about it. The tone in which he said this was rather grumpy; I realized immediately there was no point in pursuing the matter, I wouldn't get anywhere.

From this, I conclude that the Yolngu strictly protect certain areas of their culture and knowledge, and will still not surrender the content. I have mentioned earlier that the didgeridoo only became familiar to white researchers at a fairly late stage. Did the remarkable sound of this instrument not make an impression on the first explorers, or did the sound not reach them at all because it was initially concealed from them? It is also possible that in those days didgeridoos were used almost exclusively on ritual occasions where whites were not admitted.

The Australian, Gary Thomas, found out more about the subject of healing, and I will return to this later.

At any rate, whether or not the Yolngu know more about the subject of healing with sound, this special music can certainly be used for this purpose. Anyone who has opened up to the sound of the didgeridoo, has allowed themselves to be led by the sound and to feel it, will certainly have noticed that 'something' happens to him.

Music plays an important role in our life and probably no one would deny that music has a strong effect on us. This happens in a very banal, and at the same time intrusive way, in the supermarket where the soft muzak is intended to tempt us to buy things. In the past, soldiers went to war with drums and bagpipes - and nowadays, we relax after work by putting on quiet music in the evening. An understanding of the influence of music probably goes back as far as man himself. Nowadays, increasing numbers of people are taking an interest in this healing force.

Therapists particularly make use of this newly discovered ancient knowledge. Moving away from the so-called classical, analytical types of therapy, they are increasingly exploring the fields of Eastern philosophies or studying the ancient knowledge of the Indians. Therapeutic sessions certainly no longer all follow the patterns laid down by Freud and Jung. The patients are no longer placed on a couch to rake up their past by a process of making associations.

Techniques such as trance dances, breathing techniques, music, hypnosis and meditation are used to transport the patient quickly to another state of consciousness. With the help of these techniques, the patient develops an insight into what he really is, and is often able to organize his life differently on the basis of this understanding.

It still happens all too regularly that strongly analytical therapists denigrate the procedures mentioned above and describe them with the term 'shamanism', which they give a negative meaning. I would like to suggest that we should not confuse a true shaman with a quack or a charlatan. A shaman (according to the correct ancient meaning) knows exactly what he can do and what he wants to achieve with all the rituals he uses in the healing process.

In a sense, modern medics are also 'high tech' shamans. Because without the magical 'setting' - even if this consists only of equipment - there is no question of the psychosomatic effect which is generally recognized to be important. A 'contemporary' shaman who has integrated ancient and modern knowledge does not use superstition or occult hocus pocus.

It should be possible for the advantages of the various ancient and new healing methods to support each other. In this context, the didgeridoo must not be seen as a sort of magic wand in music therapy. It is much more relevant to gain a clear insight into the real possibilities which exist for applying the instrument in a meaningful way.

The descriptions given below may seem to have a rather speculative character. Some of the subjects which are discussed are difficult to substantiate scientifically, and sometimes there are insufficient practical data to provide valid proofs, i.e., proofs which can be reproduced.

In any case, I will also refer to people who have collected material about experiences with didgeridoos

The information given below is certainly not intended as a model for 'correct treatment'. It is intended particularly for those readers who have some therapeutic experience, and to encourage them to try out the possible effects of the didgeridoo themselves and find applications for it.

One of the first people who mentions the didgeridoo in connection with therapy is the psychiatrist, Dr. John Diamond. In his work he explores the relationship between health and music. In his book, 'Life Energy in Music', he describes how he sometimes teaches his students and patients to play the didgeridoo. He thinks it is beneficial for people to express themselves musically, as this generally has a positive effect on the individual's sense of well-being.

When he was looking for an instrument which a beginner could soon learn to play a little, he came across the didgeridoo. This instrument gives anyone who starts to play it complete freedom to form their own sound without any sense of coercion. Without the restrictive straightjacket of notes, complicated finger positions or difficult rhythmic patterns, it is possible to produce an astonishing range of sounds very quickly, even without mastering the technique of circular breathing.

Following an introduction to the instrument, Dr. Diamond goes on to teach the patient or student the technique of circular breathing. Mastering this technique is in itself experienced as a very positive achievement. However, the most important thing is that the player can now put aside all musical norms and create his own compositions. The pleasure which most people get from playing a didgeridoo is of great therapeutic value.

Professional musicians can also profit from playing a didgeridoo. The effect of playing the didgeridoo on a number of the acupuncture meridians which end on the lips has a very positive effect on the organism. As the lips vibrate, the meridians are constantly activated so that the energy flows easily.

In fact, Dr. Diamond uses the didgeridoo as an instrument for his patients to experience themselves.

In my view, the reference to the meridians is all the more interesting when we remember that we also 'hear' through the acupuncture system. In his book, Dr. Diamond describes why the stimulation points of the meridians act as receptors, and each produces its own response to sound and music. Meridians are often described as channels of energy running through our body which are able to assimilate 'chi' energy from outside, which is in turn distributed throughout the body.

The knowledge of this system of meridians originates from China and is used in acupuncture. When all the energy can flow in harmony everywhere, a person is healthy; if there are blocks in this flow, he becomes ill. Therefore, in China, medical science is concerned with keeping the energy flowing through the meridians or in the case of illness, starting up the flow again.

A modern therapeutic system has been developed on the basis of this theory of meridians. This is known as 'touch for health' in the 'applied kinesiology'. It uses fourteen meridians, each of which corresponds to particular organs and moods. Using a test method (muscular reflex test) which I will not describe here (there are enough books on sale and courses on this subject), it is possible to trace weakened meridians. With the help of a number of stimulation techniques these meridians can then start to flow again. In this way both spiritual and physical problems can be solved or reduced. I believe there are specific possibilities for the didgeridoo in this respect. In the context of a kinesiological test programme it could be used to bring the meridians into harmony by means of the massage which takes place when the instrument is played. Anyone who knows anything about kinesiology knows intuitively how the didgeridoo can be applied. When I talked to Dr. Diamond on this subject he had the idea that it would be possible to construct a flexible didge with a plastic hose and a funnel with a wide diameter, so that a person could try out the therapeutic treatment of the meridians on himself. Perhaps this would not be a bad way to start

Gary Thomas is the first name that springs to mind with regard to didgeridoos in Germany. Many people who play the didgeridoo in Germany learnt to do so at one of his workshops. Apart from playing at concerts Gary also uses his didgeridoo to play on people. He insists that he is not a healer, but sees himself rather as someone who makes his skills available to others. He stresses that it is important to clear the mind of all thoughts while he is playing. Otherwise he would introduce his own problems in a session intended for someone else. Every therapist should be aware of this precondition and act accordingly.

During a session Gary relies above all on his intuition and also makes use of his knowledge of the Chakras. The study of the Chakras is like an Indian version of the Chinese system of meridians. The seven main Chakras are located along the spinal column. Their task is to assimilate life energy into the body, and that is why the Chakras are often represented as funnels or spirals which enter the body in particular places.

The degree of openness and receptiveness of someone's Chakras determines that person's health. Each of these energy centres, just like the meridians, has its own characteristics and states of health and consciousness. When a certain Chakra is not active or only partly active, this has physical as well as psychological consequences. Playing the Chakras in a particular way can help them to open up. However, this treatment can only be successful if the person who is treating the patient can locate the Chakras concerned quite precisely.

In addition to the seven main Chakras, there are several other Chakras spread over the body. In his book 'Radionics and the subtle bodies of man', Dr. David Tansely expresses the possibility that these secondary Chakras correspond with the Chinese acupuncture points.

When we exchanged our experiences about playing on people, Gary described the way in which he usually works, although he certainly does not keep strictly to this method.

The person he is treating lies down and relaxes in front of him. Gary starts to play next to the left hand and slowly raises the didgeridoo in small circular movements along the arm and shoulder along the Chakra in the throat. From there he moves down the body to the pelvis and via the right leg to the foot. He then repeats the same route, but this time from the right hand to the left foot. This is the general way in which he proceeds, though he may change it, depending on the person he is treating. (Gary describes this process and other matters in an interview in the magazine *Esothera*).

Gary stressed two aspects: firstly, the slight rotating movement of the didgeridoo, and secondly, the fact that he never plays the head. His reason was that the didgeridoo is a true 'body instrument' and its vibrations would just produce chaos in the head.

Another aspect of his work which certainly deserves to be looked at by others, is playing for handicapped children. Because of its specific energy, the sound of the didgeridoo can penetrate the inner world of autistic children which is inaccessible to 'normal' people.

The same vibrating energy means that people with hearing defects can hear the music because they can feel it. The visually handicapped have an experience of spatial qualities in the sounds because of their heightened sense of hearing and feeling. This is comparable to a 'hearing kaleidoscope'.

The parents and nurses of children who suddenly behave in a way that they have never done before (laughing, dancing, crying, raging), are often astonished when this happens. On the whole children like didgeridoo music. Perhaps there are still traces in them of a time and place where they were surrounded by these sounds, i.e., in the womb.

Reports from Music Therapy

When the player is playing his patient it is important that he is aware of the fact that the sound not only 'touches' certain places on the body, but that it also evokes psychological symptoms, and not only when the Chakras or meridians are played.

In music therapy an attempt is made to change the patient's consciousness by means of sound. When the concept or state known as a 'trance' is induced in this context, this should not give rise to any misunderstanding: it certainly does not mean a state of absolute spiritual absence or 'out of the body experience'.

In the context of music therapy a trance means a state in which a person surrenders to an expanded state of consciousness and perception which can be physically experienced. In our society's system of values and boundaries which constantly control feelings and behaviour, there is little room for these sorts of experiences. However, the multi-faceted and intense nature of the experiences in a trance mean that psychotherapeutic treatment can sometimes become effective much more quickly; purely verbal, and therefore analytical therapists, are not always equally enthusiastic about this fact.

Sounds which can transport a person into this state of consciousness are known as trance-inducing sounds. From the point of music therapy there is a big difference, depending on which instrument is used to produce such a sound. One could say that every sound has its own special theme, and that every person will respond to it in his own special way. This response also depends on the images and experiences which the person

concerned has in relation to this theme, both consciously and subconsciously.
These themes are particularly those which were termed 'archetypes' by C.G. Jung. He defined these as basic patterns and primitive images which are stored in all of us and some of which are passed on from generation to generation, so that they certainly are very ancient.
In each of us this collection of patterns has approximately the same scope, though this does not mean that it is always exactly the same in every person. On the contrary, each of us imposes our own form and content on the patterns by relating them to our own experiences, needs and fears. The essence of the archetypes themselves is ultimately rather vague and intangible.
It is because of this diffuse character that archetypes can be very useful therapeutically for exposing underlying problems, particularly because their forms are not permanent but are constantly changing. Dance, music, and various forms of visual arts are suitable media for expressing archetypes insofar as this is possible. In this respect, different types of trance-inducing sounds are extremely suitable media for bringing a person or a group of people into contact with particular themes or to direct their attention to particular stories which are present in the subconscious. The choice of the instrument that is used obviously depends on the therapist's experience and preference.

In music therapy the didgeridoo is a relatively recent instrument. That is why I was glad to meet Dr. Wolfgang Strobel. He has regularly been using a didgeridoo in his psychotherapy for a number of years.
His method is characterized by the link which he establishes between the analytical, verbal method and the spiritual, physically oriented experiences. He has published extensive works on the subject, such as: 'The didgeridoo and its role in music therapy'. I have permission to quote the following examples from this work. These give a good insight into the practice of music therapy and, last but not least, contain a

number of illuminating statements about the sound made by the didgeridoo (also see bibliography).

The Didgeridoo in Receptive Music Therapy

More complex music (usually on cassette or CD) will always continue to play an important role in stimulating movement (free improvised movement or dance). The same also often applies for methods of relaxation. I hope that simple sound structures will be increasingly used in music therapy. This method of evoking changed states of consciousness on the one hand provides an opportunity for analytical techniques (because repressed material from the sub-conscious enters the daylight of consciousness), while on the other hand, it allows for new experiences, because of the energetic information which it provides, so that the range of existing forms of help can be expanded. (Cf. Strobel, 1988, 1992).

The 'trance induced by sound' which was developed by Dr. Strobel makes use of the phenomenon that the nature of a monotonous sound has a theme-related influence on what is experienced in a changed state of waking consciousness. This happens because every sound has its own energetic sound character, so that the person is conducted into an inner area of experience specifically related to this character. In this way the sound of the didgeridoo corresponds to a certain basic pattern of energy, which activates a unique psychological meaning because of its specific vibrations (sound archetype).

I will try to describe the sound archetype below, but this first requires further explanation: strictly speaking, a sound archetype should not be linked solely to the instrument, as it also depends to a great extent on the way in which the instrument is played. In all the experiences described below I am concerned with the responses to the elementary and originally monotone basic sound of the didgeridoo which is blown with the technique of circular breathing and is played without any significant modulation of tone, differentiated rhythmic structure or use of harmonics.

A few examples of experiences brought about by the didgeridoo are given below.

A middle-aged man who finds it easy to enter into the images of his own inner world, finds that he changes into a baying stag engaged in a courtship fight. He feels powerful, self-assured and archaic.

Another participant in the same group has a sensation of great power and pleasure in her stomach when she sees a herd of buffalo appearing in her mind's eye. She becomes aware of her passivity and the desire for someone to satisfy her. She does not want to do anything about this, but merely observes the herd of buffalo with a great sense of well-being, which manifests itself in her stomach as physical pleasure.

A thirty-seven-year-old woman experienced another variation of this during a sound trance workshop:

'Suddenly I was standing in the middle of a herd of buffalo. The creatures were fighting each other, or simply colliding with each other with their chests, heads and rear ends. They all behaved like real animals, keen to mate. Then I saw a wigwam which later turned into a cave, a real cave in the earth. There were some medicine men dancing around a human figure in the cave. It was .... an initiation ritual and was related to the world of women. I had a clear erotic sense of this. The ritual was for a girl who was becoming a woman. I became aware of an oppressive power and had the feeling: yes, so that is what it is like on earth. And yet I was not entirely positive about all this and felt: this is where I live, this is how I must live, it is inescapable. At some points I was the girl in the ritual, and sometimes I was outside it, looking on. What really struck me was that I did not feel any ambivalence in myself, but more a clear sense of acceptance'.

A man who had recently been struggling with a pattern of suppression in his youth - his father's kick with his father's boot and his mother's omnipotence - experienced the didgeridoo as the liberating roaring of a rutting stag. He suddenly became aware of the positive strength of his manhood, without fists hitting and boots kicking. He felt wise and strong, open-hearted and full of empathy, and his hand felt the touch of a female body...

The Sound Archetype of the Didgeridoo

Of course, archetypal images only appear to a person if that person is able to let go of his waking consciousness and submerge himself in the deeper layers of his consciousness. All the other, unspecific responses which also occur from time to time are left out of consideration here.

Any attempt at a clear description of a sound archetype is necessarily restricted, and actually robs the phenomenon of its essential nature, which must be vaguely intuitive rather than intellectually understood.

Nevertheless, I would like to try to at least give an outline of the area concerned.

For example, there are often images of powerful wild animals. Buffalo appear and elephants, a mammoth, a stag, a wild boar and a whale. The sound enables you to experience the unbridled savagery of a tiger, as well as the matriarchal power of a giant turtle.

It evokes a relationship with the element of the earth in all its variations: infinite landscapes, the violence of nature, the globe or the inside of the earth, lava. In a more symbolic form, this theme emerges as a sense of being earthed and carried by a firm base.

There is no other sound which evokes so many images from the primeval days of mankind. The mood is wild, voluptuous, vital, powerful, mighty and archaic and occasionally even rough and brutish. It refers to nature and the links with the earth, deeper instincts, sexuality and physical feelings, self-esteem and aggression, but also to the joy of life and vitality.

The physical sensation is usually concentrated in the region of the stomach or (even more often) on the pelvis and genital organs, or on the intestines or anal area. When there is a sense of potency, sexuality and sexual identity, women experience the female aspect, and men the male aspect.

Sometimes women have a proud sense of being pregnant and sometimes they even feel dragged into the powerful process of giving birth, which overwhelms them as a forceful, natural event (for example, there may be an experience of labour pains or the second stage of labour when the baby is pushed out).

There are fewer experiences of regression to the period of the person's own birth than in the case of other instruments. When such regression does take place, it is based on the sense of a safe base (which may be present or absent). For example: 'I am in the hold of a ship, I feel safe and protected', or 'I am in a hole in the ground protected by a safe wall', or even: 'I am in a narrow, shallow hollow deep under the ground. I have a sense of being imprisoned and cast out... There are lepers lying all around me, their bodies rotting and with missing limbs, neither alive or dead. There is only a little light coming through a barred window. It is terrible to be cast out in this way, imprisoned between life and death'.

Psychotherapeutic Work with the Didgeridoo

The last example clearly shows how the sound can expose deeper layers. This was the experience of an anorexic patient. Her illness was probably caused by the girl's difficult relationship with her mother which had probably existed before birth, and it expressed itself after birth in an asphyxiating relation with the mother, who did not give her a sense of physical presence or satisfy her basic sensory needs.

After working on these problematic experiences, (I don't mean using only a verbal process, but also the removal of blocks by means of catharsis), the didgeridoo can open the way to good healing experiences with its archetypal sound properties.

This is confirmed by the experience of another patient suffering from anorexia. After a long period of music therapy, she described the following experience: 'I am standing on red earth, a brownish-red field, I am dancing on the ground, stamping my feet. I am dancing to make the earth fertile. Then I squat down in a shallow depression in the earth. As I rock back and forth my menstrual blood flows into the hollow. Then I start dancing again and push all the earth back into the hollow with my feet until everything is covered and level. I feel that my hips are growing broader and my whole body is becoming fuller and rounder. I am pregnant - pregnant with the earth. I rock myself and the child in my womb. I dance and I am grateful for the fertility'.

A woman who was abused by her father and who was completely inhibited with regard to expressing her anger, found that the animal sound of the didgeridoo unleashed an attack of rage. She hurled all sorts of obscenities at me (the didgeridoo player) in a group situation: 'Filthy swine, dirty old man... you should be ashamed of yourself, I'll scratch your eyes out!'.

This aggressive breakthrough and the accompanying overcoming of her inhibitions with regard to her own aggression was the start of a new development. Gradually she was able to start on conquering the defence mechanism of her split personality and projection which she had maintained for years.

The didgeridoo is the perfect instrument for problems

related to being earthed, to the link with the earth, problems of a physical, sensory, sexual nature or related to aggression. Suppressed traumatic experiences can be relived, and if they are gone through in the right way, the positive influence of the didgeridoo becomes manifest. It has the effect of linking the person to the earth, it provides support and security, transfers vitality and strength and a positive approach to sensuality, sexuality and sexual identity.

I would like to give a brief explanation of Dr. Strobel's attempt to explain the effect of the didgeridoo.

The spectrum of sound which can be produced by the didgeridoo evokes associations with sounds perceived in the womb. Because of the common occurrence of this sort of experience, it is probable that the sense of security and the feeling of being connected to the earth, are evoked by this sound association. In addition to the sound, a major role in evoking certain associations is ascribed to the fact that the therapist plays an instrument which has an obviously phallic shape.

After lengthy practice of meditation it is common to experience inner tangible or audible vibrations (the yoga philosopher Patanjali caused this phenomenon the 'humming of the cosmic engine'). Dr. Strobel compares these vibrations with the vibrations of the didgeridoo which can be perceived with the senses: 'What is heard after a while with the inner ear when a person meditates, can be made audible for the outer ear by the didgeridoo'. You could say that by stimulating vital energy, the sound of the didgeridoo forms a firm basis, and from this basis further journeys can be undertaken into the individual's inner world.

In conclusion, I would like to quote one more excerpt from Dr. Strobel's dissertation, 'Sound, trance, healing'.

Sound does something to us. It evokes thoughts, emotions, images and physical sensations, and we do something with the sounds. We let them in or we keep them out. This is a two-way process.

Strictly speaking, it is of course not just the sound which produces this effect; it is the therapist who works with the patient via the sound, so that the patient in turn works with the therapist with his responses. What actually takes place is a completely enclosed process of interaction.

This reveals that the effect of didgeridoo music can be very profound. Above we described the result of the experiences which people in our western culture have had in just a few years of work with the didgeridoo. What a wealth of experience the Yolngu must have, for they have been using the instrument for a few thousand years!

Use of the Didgeridoo and Breathing Techniques

The didgeridoo is a wind instrument; therefore it is self-evident that like all other wind instruments, it can influence the player's breathing patterns. A special technique (circular breathing) makes the didgeridoo particularly interesting for use with breathing exercises. The pianist and breathing teacher, Gabrielle Engert-Timmermann, has therefore used the didgeridoo for some time for the positive influence on the breathing patterns of her clients.

Quite a few people have learnt to play the didgeridoo in her building and playing workshops. Mrs. Engert-Timmermann sees this part of her work as an extension of teaching music. The pure joy of playing often proves to be the first step in further explorations. It seems that remarkable things can be achieved with regard to health, both in a preventive way and during convalescence.

To return to the teaching of breathing techniques. The following interview clearly shows how the didgeridoo can be used.

Dirk: Gabi, what methods do you use when you teach breathing?

Gabi: Well, I'll have to start by telling you something about breathing in general. Usually we are not conscious of breathing. It is only when we stop breathing as a result of drastic circumstances, or start breathing faster, for example, with enjoyment or pleasure, that we notice that we are breathing at all. Thus, you could view breathing as a link between the conscious and the unconscious mind. Unlike some other bodily functions, we can control it with our will. Unfortunately, this usually means that for various different reasons we adopt ways of breathing which are counterproductive. What I try to achieve when I teach breathing could be described most accurately as: 'Waking up the pattern of breathing'. It is not aimed primarily at teaching people to breathe in the technically correct way. I think it is more important for a person to develop a sense of responsibility for himself which comes through breathing.

Dirk: What sort of people come to you for treatment?

Gabby: Most people who come to me have become aware in some way or other that the lack of energy they feel in their lives is essentially related to the way in which they breathe, although it would obviously be rather naive to view the problem of breathing as an independent phenomenon. Usually it is merely the visible, physical expression of emotional or spiritual problems.

Dirk: Do you usually use the didgeridoo with every patient, or are there certain criteria that you apply to decide on this?

Gabby: Yes, I do have some criteria. Sometimes it is enough to treat the patient and suggest exercises which enable him to experience breathing as an original basic force. This can in itself change his breathing pattern. I use the didgeridoo for people who have problems which are closely related to breathing, or problems related to eroticism, being open to the world, giving and taking, setting boundaries. For them, I always play the didgeridoo at the start or at the end of the treatment. As soon as I have the feeling that the sound has been 'accepted', I try to persuade the patient to learn to play it himself.

Dirk: What, in your opinion, is the effect of teaching this?

Gabby: It would be better to ask: ' Why is it so good for a person?' I think it is because everyone who plays the didgeridoo will sooner or later find his 'own' theme. This starts with the stimulation of the diaphragm, which the Greeks called the 'seat of the soul'. In proportion to the degree to which the diaphragm is activated when you play the didgeridoo, it is possible to break down inner blocks. Anyone who learns the techniques of circular breathing will sooner or later experience that it is possible to breathe in a certain rhythm, so that the emphasis is on breathing out. Teaching breathing is aimed almost entirely at the practice of this technique of breathing out. In this connection I would like to emphasize that the quality of breathing out determines the way in which you breathe in. And what about the nose? When you play, you can only breathe in through the nose. Everyone knows that it is healthier to breathe through the nose, and thus it is an excellent way of practising this.

Dirk: There are some specific complaints of the respiratory passages, such as asthma. Can you use the didgeridoo for this?

Gabby: I think you can, but I've only just started working on that. With regard to those sorts of complaints, I would just like to say in general: What is my attitude to life?'. Thus, with regard to someone who suffers from asthma, it is a matter of concentrating on letting go or surrendering. From a medical point of view, the didgeridoo is an interesting instrument in this sort of case. Very simply, asthma patients do not have any problems breathing in, but they find it very difficult to get the air they have taken in back out because their bronchia are furred up and stuck together, and that is why they cannot take in any more fresh air.

Completely instinctively, they try and ease this condition by using the so-called lip brake. To do this, they press their lips together when they breathe out. The resistance causes the air pressure in the bronchia to increase so that they are pushed open and are cleared for breathing out. Exactly the same thing happens when you play the didgeridoo: you constantly breathe out against the resistance of the compressed lips. Therefore, the bronchia have a sort of recovery break while the patient continues to play. The experience of breathing effortlessly at the same time as making music must have a positive effect !

Dirk: Is it really so easy to play the didgeridoo - I mean doesn't the difficulty of mastering the technique cancel out the beneficial effect of playing?

Gabi: My building and playing courses have shown that there is no fundamental obstacle to learning to play the didgeridoo. People with chronic breathing problems may find it more difficult at first, but if they stop in time and do not put themselves under too much strain, they will keep advancing. The didgeridoo is an instrument which cannot be 'mastered' with ambition and will. I have often found that people with purely selfish motives are the ones who are unable to get on with the didge. Most do not even manage to produce a key note. You must be prepared to surrender all your strength and concentration to the instrument and let go of all the old patterns of thinking. It is only then that you find how the sound can gradually change into a pure and joyful experience.

Dirk: When you are concerned with therapies which emphasize the physical experience, the principle of consciously organized hyperventilation constantly comes up. Is there a link with the didgeridoo?

Gabi: That's something you should ask a doctor. Perhaps someone would like to do some research in that field. As you know, the carbon dioxide in the blood falls when you breathe in the way that causes hyperventilation. This in turn produces a lower calcium level, resulting in the well-known symptoms: cramps, intense experiences at other levels of consciousness, etc. In fact, the composition of the blood changes drastically. As far as I know, this does not happen when you play the didgeridoo. Breathing in and breathing out are balanced in a healthy way. I often play for half an hour at a stretch, and I have never noticed the slightest trace of hyperventilation, no matter how intensely I play. However, I could imagine that, like jogging, it produces more adrenaline or other substances which produce a feeling of euphoria, but that is pure speculation. But as I said, the didgeridoo has a very refreshing influence on life energy and a scientific explanation is not always necessary for this.

Part 4

A Tale
from
the Dreamtime

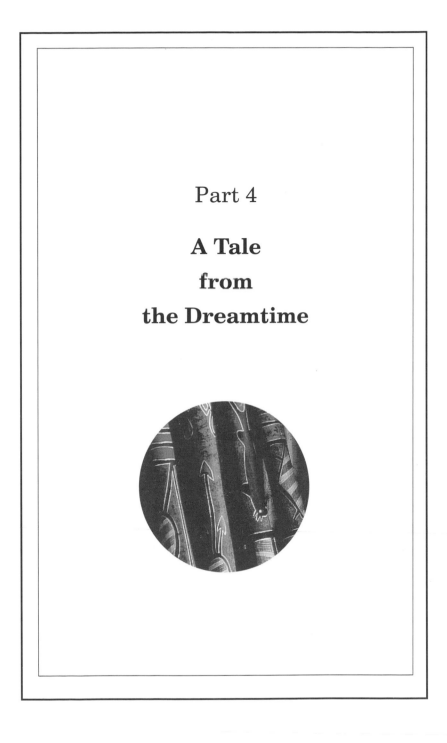

Meeting Bill Harney

Before we go on to the more practical side of playing the didgeridoo, in this part I would like to make a little excursion into the Dreamtime.

Of course, there are several different stories about the creation of the didgeridoo, but in the next few pages I would like to relate Bill Harney's version .

Bill is one of those didgeridoo makers who tries to live a life which is somewhere between the two cultures. Nevertheless, he feels a close link with the land of his ancestors, and he is convinced that he must look after this. He calls it 'looking after the country'.

Bill does not live only from his craft products. He also organizes tours, two or three days long, through the land of the 'Brothers of Lightning'. It is certainly worth going on one of these tours. Bill is a born storyteller, and on the road he talks a lot about his people and the Dreamtime. Bill comes from the Wardaman language group. The story related below is part of a recording which I made. He not only told the story, but he sang from time to time to give me an impression of the way in which the heroes from the Dreamtime behaved. His songs and the way he played the didgeridoo were very similar.

I've given phonetic equivalents of the terms he used from his own language.

'In this country you find many didgeridoos. That is because of the birds. In the past, in the Dreamtime, birds were people just like us. They carried everything they had – which was very little – with them. They tied it around their waist, carried it on their shoulders, or took it under their arm. Such as, for example, the boomerangs or diggers. One of these birds, which is known now as the 'long-tailed fashion', was the didgeridoo player in those times. In our language it was called Giddabush. It always carried its didge with it, and when it was not playing it tied it firmly around its hips.

Later, the Giddabush bird had a long tail which always reminds us that he was the didgeridoo player.

Another bird, the Butcher bird, was also a human in the Dreamtime. He discovered all the different sorts of wood, and used some of these as clapsticks. Because he had a fine voice he became the singer. You can hear that nowadays because he is still a good singer as a bird.

The third bird I want to tell you about is the Piwi (Australian Magpie-Lark). He painted himself with black and red earth and became the dancer.

So, Giddabush was the blower and discovered the didgeridoo, Butcher bird sang and used the clapsticks, and Piwi danced.

While they were playing, singing and dancing, they gave everything a name and this is how things were created: the mountains, the trees, the grass – they named everything!

When they rested, they hid under a shady tree. To make sure that they did not die of hunger, they regularly went hunting. Then they would make a fire in a hollow in the earth, and would roast their catch over the fire.

As soon as they had had enough to eat and had rested, they started on their work again: playing the didgeridoo, singing and dancing to create the world in this way. When they had finished, they said to each other: 'Now we will pass everything on, the didgeridoo, the clapsticks, the songs and the dances'.

And this is what has happened ever since, from generation to generation.

This was the history of Giddabush, Butcher bird, who is known as Golbornan in our language, and Magpie, who we call Glededaa'.

Bill Harney

Part 5

The Infinite Sound

The Blowing Technique

Anyone who wants to play the didgeridoo obviously has to have an instrument. I will say more about making or buying an instrument in the next chapter. We will first examine the technique of playing it.

The breathing technique which is used for blowing on the didgeridoo is sometimes described as circular breathing, but in fact this term is not altogether correct.

The breathing technique for playing the didgeridoo concentrates on breathing out. By controlling the breath in a very special way, the air which is breathed out is blown through the lips in an uninterrupted flow.

This blowing technique, or rather breathing technique, is not a special discovery of the ancient people of Australia. The technique has been known for several thousand years in Asia, Africa and Europe. The aulo players (an aulo is a sort of double flute) in ancient Greece used this technique, and it was also known to the Ancient Egyptians.

In the past, the bourdon (an uninterrupted key note which carries the melody) was a common musical device. We are still familiar with this principle in the bagpipes and hurdy-gurdy. When you wish to express the 'infinite nature' of such a note on a wind instrument, it is possible only using a breathing technique which involves constantly breathing out.

In Europe, the interest in the bourdon gradually disappeared after the Middle Ages. In Eastern music, the ?Bourdon is still a traditional element, and therefore this breathing technique is still used. In Europe, only oboe players still learn the technique of always breathing out. Musicians who use this way of playing on other instruments (flute, trumpet, trombone) were, until recently, considered rather strange and made their audience feel rather out of breath by producing notes which went on for minutes on end. 'When on earth is he going to breathe again?' Nevertheless, circular breathing is once again attracting interest. Nowadays there are even composers who expressly indicate that their pieces must be played using this technique. In fact, this breathing technique was used not only in music; glass blowers and goldsmiths also used it in their work. Goldsmiths used their breath to produce a constant supply of oxygen for the flame of their soldering equipment. Glass blowers need a very constant air pressure to create their works. Thus, it is clear that the system of circular breathing is a skill which can be used in many ways, and in fact anyone can master this skill with a bit of patience.

What actually happens in circular breathing ?
While the air is blown out into an instrument, the player keeps a little bit of air in his cheeks just before using up all the air in his lungs. Before he breathes out through the nose, the back part of the throat is closed off by pressing the back of the tongue against the soft part of the palate. When it is 'sealed', the player can breathe in through the nose, and at the same time slowly press out the air he has saved up with the muscles of his cheek. Breathing in through the nose and pressing the air out of the mouth happens at the same time. Once the lungs have been filled up again, the tongue is relaxed, the back of the throat opens up and the player goes back to breathing out through the lungs.
The skill lies in keeping the pressure with which the air is pressed out between the lips at exactly the same level, even when switching from breathing out with the lungs, to breathing out with the cheeks. As soon as there is any change in this pressure, it can be heard in the volume or intensity of the note.

Of course, it is all very well to describe it in this way, but this is easier said than done.
I will therefore give a few exercises which make all this easier,

and which are fun in themselves, particularly because they allow us to do things which we were never allowed to do before, like spitting in water, blowing bubbles with a straw in a glass full of water ...
When I do these exercises it always reminds me of very boring visits to restaurants in my youth, when I tried to pass the time with these sorts of tricks.
Sometimes children want to learn to play the didgeridoo. When I try to explain to them what they have to do with their mouth to seal off the back of the throat, they soon look bored. I thought of a sentence which would help them to feel the technique. When you say it, you constantly use that part of your throat which you need to separate breathing out with the cheeks with breathing out with the lungs: 'Giggly girls go great guns on grand gardens'. For every 'g', the back of the tongue has to be pressed against the soft part of the palette.

Here are the exercises 'step by step'.

1. Blow out the cheeks and try to build up some pressure in the cavity of the mouth. To start with, you may wish to pinch your nose.
If you find it difficult to blow out your cheeks you may find it easier to start by blowing up a few balloons.

2. Keep your cheeks blown up, then try breathing normally in and out through the nose, while the cheeks remain blown up.

3. Perhaps the best place to do the next exercise is in the bath, over a wash basin or outside.
Fill your mouth with water so your cheeks are completely full. Again breath in and out through the nose.
As you keep breathing, press out the water through your lips in a thin stream, using your cheeks to put pressure on the water. You will soon find that these two apparently conflicting movements can be carried out at the same time very well.
For the next mouthful of water, push out a jet while you are just breathing in through the nose.

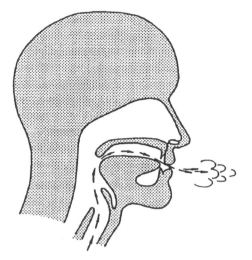

Stage 1
Breathing out with the lungs.

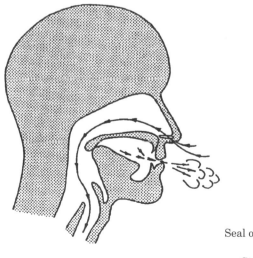

Stage 2
Seal off the mouth cavity
from the throat.
Start pressing the air
out of the cheeks.
At the same time breathe in through the nose.

This exercise seems to be very effective because the water makes sure you can feel what is happening much more easily than when your mouth is empty.

4. Repeat exercise 3, but this time without water.
Wet your lips with your tongue, blow up your cheeks full of air, press out the air, and at the same time breathe in through the nose!

5. Now it is a matter of putting together the various steps which have been practised separately so that they form a continuous cycle.
In other words: press out the air in your lungs, build up a supply of air in your cheeks, seal off the throat with the back of the tongue, and at the same time start to press out the air saved in the cheeks while you are breathing in through the nose. Once the lungs are filled up again, carefully change over to breathing out from the lungs, and so on ...

6. One way of practising this whole cycle is with the help of a glass of water and a straw. Don't use a thin lemonade straw, but the thicker sort, such as those used for milkshakes.
Put the straw in the water and bubble up the water by blowing the straw. Now use the technique which you practised in the previous stages; keep the water bubbling constantly. You can see exactly how regular your circular breathing is from the way in which the air bubbles rise up.
If there is not enough resistance when you are blowing into the water, so that the supply of air in your cheeks has been pushed out too quickly, squash the straw a little or start with a thinner straw. A greater resistance makes the changeover from breathing out with the cheeks to breathing out with the lungs, much easier.
Most people enjoy this exercise, particularly in workshops when at least ten people are practising together and the participants have the feeling they are in a large aquarium. It can give rise to a great deal of hilarity.
As you master the new technique, it's a matter of reducing the

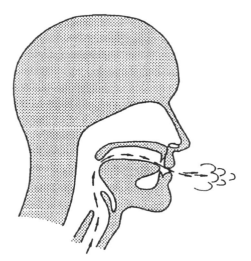

Stage 3
Stop breathing in,
and press
the remaining air out.

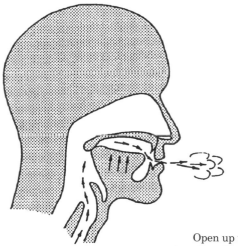

Stage 4
Open up the throat and change
from breathing out with the cheeks
to breathing out with the lungs.
This completes the cycle
and you are back to stage 1.

resistance and practising with thicker straws. After all, a didgeridoo has a wider opening, and it does not contain any water, so the resistance is very low.

Once you have mastered circular breathing on the didgeridoo, you can also practice it on a recorder or another instrument. With a little practice, this can be achieved.

For musicians who want to learn to play another wind instrument and master the circular breathing technique, the didgeridoo is an ideal instrument for practising.

On Kangaroos and Dingos: the Playing Technique

An aspiring player can produce his first notes on the didgeridoo long before he despairs of learning the technique of circular breathing, and loses all his enthusiasm for the venture because it involves so much practice. It is fairly easy to produce a key note. In order to continue enjoying playing as well as practising and progressing in both areas, it is best to alternate breathing techniques and blowing the key note.

Assuming that you have a sound didgeridoo, producing the first note will not really be a problem. For example, it is not necessary for the player to learn to apply great pressure with his lips, as for a trumpet, before he can produce a good sound. With a didgeridoo, the player flutters his lips. You may have done this when you were a child; otherwise you have probably heard other children doing it, imitating the sound of a car. The air is loosely blown through soft lips: 'Brrrrummmm'; and you can splutter. When you make this sound, with a much longer flow of air, this is exactly the movement of the lips required to play a didgeridoo.

Obviously the player presses his lips against the mouthpiece of his instrument when he plays. There are two possible different positions.

1. *The central position*: The mouthpiece is placed at the middle of the mouth against the cleft in the upper lip, so that the vibration of the lips takes place from this central point.

2. *The sideways position*: The mouthpiece is placed against the side of the mouth, so that the lips vibrate on one side from the cleft in the middle of the lips to the corner of the mouth on the left or right. Personally, I prefer the central position; I think it is easier to produce the different types of sound in this way.

When you start to experiment with your didgeridoo, it's important to find out what's best for you. Therefore, change the pressure of your mouth against the opening of the didgeridoo in different ways, and also press your lips together in different ways: stiffly pressed, softly pouting, and everything in between. You will soon find that not much force is needed to produce a key note. In fact, it is important not to blow too hard. At first you might produce all sorts of 'rude' noises, but increasingly you will find you are producing the true characteristic didgeridoo sound. Once you have discovered how you can blow this sound again and again, you can start practising the circular breathing when you are blowing. 'Never mind', everything takes its time.

Practising can be much more fun when you make variations in the sound. You can do this by enlarging or reducing the size of the mouth cavity by moving your tongue or using your uvula or throat (singing, talking, groaning). A real rolling tongued 'r' also produces a special effect.

Once you have succeeded in producing the 'real' sounds with your didgeridoo, it's a good idea to put the instrument aside and start from on circular breathing again. Then, when you have experimented with all the sounds you can make on your didgeridoo, you can gradually start to apply the circular breathing technique as you are blowing. The special thing about playing a didgeridoo is that the instrument teaches you how to do it as you practice: 'Learning by doing'.

Once you have measured the technique of circular breathing, you will be surprised how little air is needed to keep the sound going.

To develop a varied playing technique it is important to learn to use your breath economically. Breathing is the first thing a baby does when he is born. If he does not start breathing straightaway, he is given a sharp rap on his behind and gets the message immediately: 'Come on !' In some tribes who live closer to nature than we do, newborn babies have life blown into them through the mouth or nose – this is a much gentler invitation to taking their first breath. At any rate, from the moment that we first breathe air into our lungs, we pay hardly any attention to our breathing.

And yet, breathing properly is a real art. This is evident from the fact that so many people suffer from conditions which are caused by an incorrect way of breathing. In countries such as Japan, Tibet, China and India, there have been breathing schools since ancient times. At these schools the emphasis is placed on a conscious method of breathing which removes or prevents all sorts of complaints resulting from breathing in the wrong way. These physical processes of consciousness, like spiritual consciousness, form part of the philosophical beliefs in those countries; for example, Hatha Yoga, the method of spiritual and physical consciousness which was developed in India and has become increasingly well-known here.

The system of circular breathing develops our feeling for a more aware method of breathing. Thus it intuitively becomes simpler to co-ordinate the different steps in breathing better.

In simple terms, we use two different cavities in the body for 'normal' breathing: the chest cavity and the abdominal cavity. This means that there is a difference between breathing from the chest and breathing from the abdomen. Most people breathe almost exclusively from their chest. This 'superficial' breathing results in an extremely impoverished supply of fresh air and removal of used air.

It is much more effective to combine chest and abdominal breathing. Normally the abdominal breathing automatically alternates with chest breathing. We breathe from the top to the bottom in an automatic undulating movement.

The diaphragm ('a' in the illustration) regulates abdominal breathing. It is part of the system of abdominal muscles which regulates breathing, but has the most important function: it

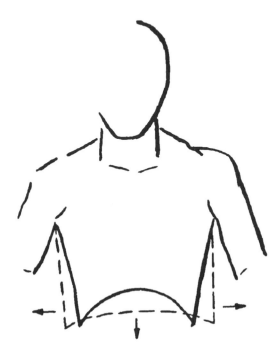

regulatcs breathing in (2) by itself, and is also the most active of all the abdominal muscles with regard to breathing out (1). In normal breathing the diaphragm accounts for approximately 60% of the air displacement. In this way it performs a leading role in all the physical functions which are related to breathing. The diaphragm is a muscular membrane which seals off the entire chest cavity at the bottom, and forms an elastic wall separating the chest cavity from the abdominal cavity. When it is relaxed, it is like a sort of dome in the chest cavity. When it contracts the dome seems to 'collapse', the diaphragm moves down and straightens out so that the chest cavity becomes larger in the vertical plane.

(Taken from Werner Richter, Bewusste Flötentechnik)

All this is easy to see from the outside because the body visibly moves out at the waist when the diaphragm contracts. The organs in the abdominal cavity, (stomach, intestines, etc.) are slightly compressed. This has a slight massaging effect on them, which in turn has a good effect on our well-being. When we breathe out, all the abdominal muscles are involved.

According to the latest ideas, it is not possible to train the diaphragm directly. It is subject to an involuntary respiration system and can therefore not be controlled by our conscious will. In this way it is comparable to the heart which can also be trained indirectly, for example, by sport. The clearest way of demonstrating how the diaphragm works is shown when we cough, yawn, laugh or hiccough. In fact, the contraction of the abdominal muscles has little influence on the movement of the diaphragm, except that it supports these movements. Thus there is no point in doing special exercises for the abdominal muscles with the idea of actively influencing the movement of the diaphragm. The only way in which we can train the combined abdominal and chest respiration is by consciously breathing in this way, not only when we are practising, but all day long. The Greeks thought of the diaphragm as the seat of the soul; they used the same word for the spirit, consciousness and diaphragm.

If you want to know more about abdominal breathing, do the following exercise. First, breathe in with your back straight and without pulling it in. This is sometimes called breathing from the pelvis. Then bend your back forwards, fold your arms around your stomach, and again try to breathe from the pelvis. There is a noticeable difference in breathing capacity; this immediately shows that the position of the body has a great influence on the capacity to play the didgeridoo.

For me, one of the best positions for playing the didgeridoo is the position which the Aborigines use themselves. The player sits on the ground with one leg bent to the side and one leg stretched forwards, quite relaxed.The foot of the stretched out leg helps to support the didgeridoo (see illustration). You certainly should not sit with your back bent ! If this position gives you backache because the muscles in your back are not

used to it, it helps to rock softly to and fro as you are playing. This means that the muscles alternately relax and contract, and avoids tension. Playing in a standing position has the great disadvantage that the neck is bent relatively too far forward, and this will eventually lead to problems. Alternatively it is also possible to sit on a chair. In this case, the didge must be supported with a foot.

Now that we have devoted some attention to breathing and the position of the body, it's time to look at the way in which different sounds are made.

Alice Moyle from the Australian Institute for Aboriginal and Torres Straits Islanders Studies, in Canberra, pointed out that in fact not enough attention is devoted to an aspect of the technique for playing the didgeridoo which is very important. This concerns the pronunciation of words while playing. Many of the rhythms played on the didgeridoo are created because words are spoken or even sung as the player is blowing. This changes the character of the sound; if words such as 'didjamoo', 'ritoru' or 'didgeridoo' are pronounced in a constant rhythm and articulated as clearly as the vibrating lips allow, this produces sounds with an almost meditative effect. A didgeridoo used in this way can be of great value in elocution lessons.

In order to prepare for producing different sounds, we will examine the stomach once again. Some of the sounds described below require increased breathing pressure and the diaphragm has to be supported by the abdominal muscles.

The following exercise will help you to feel exactly what we mean. Fill your lungs with air as deeply as possible, breathing right down into the abdominal cavity. Then press your hands onto your waist and push out the air in bursts by powerfully pulling in the abdominal muscles. At the same time, blow the air out through your mouth, with your lips lightly closed, so that you clearly hear the breath coming out in puffs 'pfft – pfft'. Do not practice this exercise too long or you might find that it gives you painful cramps.

The first sounds to practise on your didgeridoo are the sounds created when you clearly articulate an 'A or OU' while you are playing. If you still have problems with the co-ordination of the circular breathing technique, forget about this at first. The use of the speaking technique while you are playing opens up whole new areas of resonance in the body, but it does require more air. This can be heard immediately from the tone produced in this way, which becomes fuller and louder. Once you're able to produce both sounds separately you can also try blowing them alternately; A – OU – A – OU. This is your first rhythm !

If you do this making use of the circular breathing technique, the rhythm is even further emphasized. It is not possible to speak during the stage at which you breathe out with the cheeks, because the sound is formed in another way and therefore has a different tone. The more you practise the quicker these changes merge. Eventually, breathing out with the cheeks no longer causes a noticeable break, but becomes a stylistically useful variation.

In fact, it is possible to learn to speak the whole alphabet in this way while you are playing; it is a good exercise for learning to form sounds and for getting to know the possibilities of the didgeridoo.

There is an infinite variation of possible sounds. A number of these which are often used have their own meaning and name. I would like to describe four of them on the following pages, although it is in itself a difficult task to describe sounds using words. I have therefore included a pictogram with every description. The basis of each sound described here is the key note which is constantly produced. It is shown in the pictogram by the dotted bar at the bottom. The different sound variations are modulated on this. In order to form the individual sound values you use the so-called falsetto, which is made at the top of the throat when the larynx is constricted. The description of the sounds I have given here is my first attempt to reproduce them. Actually, it is best to learn these things by listening to a number of recordings and trying to imitate what you have heard, or by joining in one of the workshops which are sometimes held even in our own country. Everyone should try to create their own style, because we would never be able to approach the sound which the Yolngu themselves make. A useful tip is to run some water through the didgeridoo before playing it. This can often improve the sound. The Yolngu often wash their didgeridoo for hours on end before they start playing. There is no risk that the wood will split.

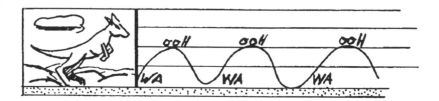

The Kangaroo

This sound is most like that made by the jew's harp. The back of the tongue is pressed up against the soft part of the palate. By increasing and decreasing the size of the mouth cavity, you can create a note which 'hops up and down', and is reminiscent of a kangaroo hopping over the key note.

The true rhythm of this way of playing can be learnt best by looking at some kangaroos hopping about. A nature film about Australian fauna could help to get your imagination going. After all, the imagination and dreams are always an important precondition for playing the didgeridoo.

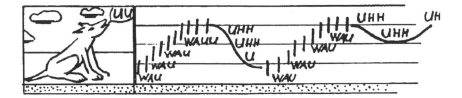

The Dingo

Dingos are the wild dogs of Australia. They were almost exterminated by white farmers because they sometimes attacked sheep which were old and weak. It has now been shown quite clearly that they were never a real threat to the sheep population, but their rarity means that there is a sad lack in the ecological balance. Imitating the sound of the dingo starts with barking while you are playing, and the barking then changes into the howling of a wolf. You will not manage this without the help of your abdominal muscles. Make sure that you keep vibrating your lips.

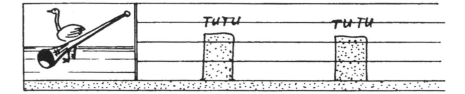

The Trombone Sound

As the name suggests, this is a sound which is like the sound of a trumpet, or even more, of a trombone. You have to purse your lips and then keep them tightly pressed together, in the way that a trombonist plays, and then the air is powerfully expelled from the abdomen. A great deal of practice is required to assimilate this technique in your normal playing without a break. It is easier with a narrow mouthpiece, or even a didgeridoo with a smaller diameter than usual. The short double sound, 'TOO TOO', indicates a change in the rhythm of traditional music or the end of a song. It also imitates the sound made by the emu, the Australian ostrich. The words Yiraki, Yiki-Yiki or Yiraga mean the neck of an emu or merely a neck, and are often used as other names for the didgeridoo ! You can produce a really jazzy sound when you learn to alternate the key note and the trombone sound rapidly so that a percussive style results.

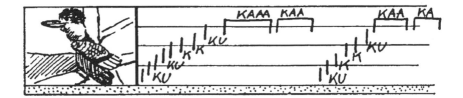

The Kookaburra

Kookaburras are found almost all over Australia. These birds are also known by the popular names 'laughing Hans' and 'King of the Bush'. The kookaburra mocks anyone who tries to creep through the bush but makes a huge racket.

It is quite difficult to imitate its song on the didge. A great deal of air and a lot of 'abdominal support' are required to produce the appropriate sound.

As regards the pitch of the note, the imitation starts in the middle regions and then moves up to the higher regions. This can only be achieved by using the larynx. The first syllables are short and seem to be cut off, but towards the end they become longer and longer 'cuccacoo, cuckoo, cacacacuckoo, cacaa, caa, caaa, caaaaaaa!' Obviously the key note has to keep sounding at the same time.

The Didgeridoo from a Theoretical Point of View

Didgeridoos are wind instruments. In this section they are most closely related to the trombone and the bugle. The sound they produce is about 90dB, which is comparable to a low note on a trumpet.

The blowing technique is the same as that used for a trombone: a column of air is vibrated by vibrating the lips. Only about one percent of the mechanical energy used for playing is converted into sound energy.

The 'boring' is sometimes slightly conical, but usually more or less cylindrical. The pitch of a didgeridoo is determined by its length and the extent to which the tube is, or is not, conical. This is clear when we compare a clarinet and an oboe.

The boring of a clarinet is mainly cylindrical. When it is 'overblown', this produces a note which is twelve notes higher than the key note. This interval is known as a twelfth.

An oboe, which has a boring almost just as long as that of the clarinet, but with a conical shape, has a key note which is an octave higher. When the oboe is overblown, it produces an interval of an octave.

Two didgeridoos with the same length, but one of which has an end one third larger than the other, can therefore differ a whole note in pitch. When a didgeridoo is overblown, this means that it produces a trombone-like sound, and this note is between a seventh and an eleventh above the key note.

The key notes of most didgeridoos are in the region A, B, C, D, E, F, and the semitones between these. One of the most striking properties of the didgeridoo is that certain frequencies with the related harmonics can be produced without any changes in the loudness of the volume or pitch. This special spectrum of sounds lies between 500 and 2,500 Hz. It is produced solely by using the mouth cavity in different ways, just as for singing harmonics. At the same time the key tone of 60 – 80 Hz simply sounds on. The higher frequencies can always be heard above this.

One factor which is very important in determining the sound is the fact that the player sings into the didgeridoo. The open throat produces a harmonic which cannot be heard in normal singing. In principle, it is possible to sing any note, because the path from the larynx to the lips or from the lips to the vibrating column of air in the pipe has virtually no return. Usually, the player sings a tenth, because this creates a powerful lower octave which is rich in harmonics. The sound produced with this interval at the moment at which the voice is suddenly added to the key note, is sometimes reminiscent of the 16 pedal register of an organ.

Gliding notes and falsetto are also used, for example, to imitate animal noises. If a fifth is sung instead of a tenth, this produces a weaker lower octave. In this case, the note that is sung is already low and therefore it can only be sung fairly softly.

The rhythm of the notes mentioned above is produced mainly by pressing the tongue against the teeth or the palate to form letters. This can be a single beat (e.g., dah, dah, dah). A double beat (e.g. dah kah, dah kah), and a triple beat (dakadah, dakadah, dakadah).

In 'classical' didgeridoo music there are a number of different rhythmic patterns. In the free rhythms the didgeridoo moves entirely independently of the singer's beat, which is tapped out with clapsticks; it is set in another time. The polyrhythmic style of playing is very common. In this case the didgeridoo player plays a rhythm with two beats, while the singer sings three beats in the same time. Apparently, completely contradictory rhythmic figures can be produced by the use of syncopation. Syncopation involves a rhythmic accent: in the rhythm the emphasis is placed just next to the actual beat. This style of playing produces a physical tension or relaxation in the listener, depending on the way in which it is applied. The unexpected emphasis on the volume or length of beats which are not normally accented, forms the essence of the rhythmic pattern and determines whether or not it is an inspiring experience. A didgeridoo player can only consider himself to be good when he has mastered this technique.

Part 6

Your Own
Instrument

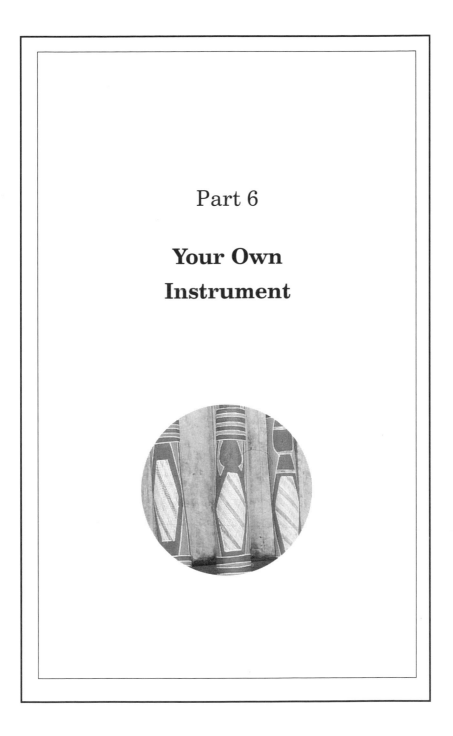

Making your Own Didgeridoo

Unfortunately – or perhaps it is fortunate – there are no termites in our woods which hollow out tree trunks and branches as they do in Australia. Therefore, you will have to find a substitute if you want to make your own didgeridoo. Fortunately, there is plenty of choice: bamboo, wood, synthetic materials and aluminium pipes are all suitable. If you are as unfussy as your didgeridoo as the original inventors, even a PVC pipe will do. For an Aborigine, the sound of the instrument is much more important than its aesthetic appearance. However, anyone who wants their didgeridoo to look good as well, can certainly go to town when he makes his own instrument. Obviously, this depends on his carpentry skills, but there is no reason why he shouldn't produce a masterpiece of wood turning.

If you want to keep it simpler, there is a choice between two useful materials.

Synthetic Fibre Pipes

It is quickest to make a didgeridoo with the end of a synthetic or acrylic pipe such as those used for drainage pipes. There are black pipes and grey pipes which are sold by the metre in plumbing shops as well as in the better D.I.Y. shops. In fact, it is worth keeping an eye on building sites: when water pipes and heating pipes are laid, there are often some remnants which may be thrown away, though they could be just long enough for a didgeridoo. It's always worth asking.

It is possible to produce an acceptable sound with a pipe with a

Rock drawing of a
non-human player.

Seated player holding his
didge with both hands.

diameter of 40 mm and walls 3 mm thick. The first didge you make should not be longer than 110 cm or 120 cm at the most. Later on, you can start experimenting with longer pipes. There is a particular ceremony which uses an extremely long didgeridoo, and the player lies on his side on the ground.

The didgeridoo player, Alan Dargin, made a recording using a synthetic pipe in which he produced one of the lowest notes ever made by a musician. When you have found a suitable synthetic pipe, you merely sand the ends smooth and slightly rounded with a file. Then polish the material with fine sandpaper, and your didgeridoo is ready. If the mouthpiece is too wide, you can make it narrower with beeswax in the traditional manner, and adapt it to the anatomical structure of your lips. I will describe how to make a mouthpiece in more detail below.

Bamboo

In my opinion, the best substitute for eucalyptus is bamboo. This is sold in any well-stocked garden centre. In Australia it is also used for didgeridoos, particularly in those areas where it grows naturally. David Blanasi often used the word 'bamboo' when he meant didgeridoo. Alice M. Moyle's research showed that in the past, bamboo was often the material used. On some rock drawings the didgeridoo players are holding the instruments in one hand. This indicates that it is a light material (see the illustrations opposite and on the next page). They were copied from rock drawings and were used to illustrate an article by Alice M. Moyle in the magazine, *World Archaeology*, Volume 3, No. 1981, which kindly made the drawings available for this book.

Bamboo really would be ideal if it did not eventually crack. It is a natural material and feels more comfortable than aluminium or plastic. The cracks develop eventually because of the difference in tension resulting from the expansion of the porous inside of the pipe resulting from moisture (condensed breath) while the outside remains dry, and cannot resist the pressure from inside.

Player, holding his didge with
one hand, which suggests that it is
made of a light material, such as bamboo.

Standing didgeridoo player holding his
instrument with both hands.

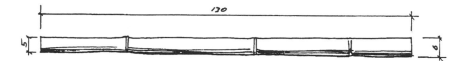

How to make the Didgeridoo

The pipe is sawn off at a length of 120-160 cm. It should have a diameter between 35 and 60 mm. Usually, bamboo tapers slightly. In that case, it is self-evident that the narrow end becomes the mouthpiece.

**The ideal tool
for making a didgeridoo:
a rasp on a broomstick.**

Ideal state:
Bill Harney's supply of didges.
The wheel axle at the front on the right fits
perfectly in this nonchalant picture.

At the places where there are buds in the bamboo, the edges have to be removed. It is best to do this with a pointed iron rod. But even when these transverse layers have been broken and scraped away as far as possible, remnants remain in the inside wall which are an obstacle to making a good sound. It is best to make the tools yourself for removing these irregularities. A rasp without its handle can be attached to a broomstick with two jubilee clips. This means that the tool is long enough to remove all the irregularities, even in fairly long pipes (see previous page for illustration). Returning to the subject of 'cracks': obviously the swelling of the porous inside of the bamboo can be prevented by sealing it with a sealer. For example, the inside of alpine horns are treated with so-called resinous varnish. If you decide to varnish the inside, make sure that the solvent used in the varnish has properly evaporated. Water-based varnish should be applied in several thin layers, and every layer must be quite dry before the next layer is applied, otherwise the moisture could still suddenly cause the inside of the pipe to swell up.

Another possibility is to use beeswax. In this case the wax must be dissolved in benzine so that it can easily be applied in a thin layer. To do this, some beeswax is placed in a clean tin and heated until it melts (e.g., in a pan of hot water). The liquid wax is then mixed with benzine. **Never do this near a naked flame!** Do not try this on a cooker (even on an electric cooker) where the wax was heated. The wax will remain liquid long enough so that you can take it somewhere where you can work with it quite safely.

Beforehand, you should have tied an old (cotton) rag to a long stick. This is used to spread the liquid wax mixture as evenly and thoroughly as possible on the inside of the bamboo pipe. When the benzine has evaporated, a hard layer of pure beeswax remains. It is also possible to take measures on the outside to prevent the bamboo cracking.

In the first place, it is possible to roast the bamboo carefully over a fire. Many players swear by this technique and say that nothing else is necessary.

Alpine horns are wrapped with so-called shiny tape along their entire length. Slightly moistened raffia or reeds can also be used for this purpose. If you wrap your didgeridoo from top to bottom in this way there is no need to worry about cracks.

Moreover, I have found that it is actually sufficient to wrap only the two ends of the bamboo pipe. Before you start wrapping it, the smooth outer wall should be roughly sanded so that the glue will stick. Then water-resistant wood glue is spread on the sanded area, and the material being used is wrapped on the glue. I secure the beginning and the end of the wrapping material with elastic (any wide elastic will do). Once the glue has set, the ends which are not wrapped are cut off and the wrapped part is finished off with transparent varnish.

Finally, the mouthpiece has to be made. This is done with beeswax. I would never use any other sort of wax. It might contain components which could be damaging to your health because they are in constant contact with your lips.

A friend of mine in Australia had a simple solution for determining the size of the mouthpiece: he said it had to be the same size as a 20 cent coin. Unfortunately, we do not usually have these coins here, and so we will calculate the size in mm. The opening of the mouthpiece should be between 25 and 30 mm. At first, a rather narrow opening makes it much easier to blow. Once the player's skill increases and he has mastered several variations, he will automatically want to enlarge the size of the opening.

The beeswax is softly kneaded by hand, and is then used to form a small 'snout' which joins diagonally onto the wall of the inside without any transition. A slightly oval mouthpiece is most suited to the shape of the lips. Eventually, you will discover the shape which suits you best. Every mouth has a different shape, and therefore every mouth requires a different mouthpiece.

Many people do not like mouthpieces made of wax; they are rather grubby and unhygienic. If you know how to turn wood, you can turn your own mouthpiece from the wood of a fruit tree.

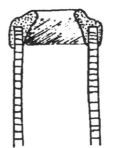

**A mouthpiece
made of beeswax.**

It is also possible to cut the mouthpiece from a piece of wood. This sort of mouthpiece is simply stuck onto the instrument with beeswax. If you are considering doing this with some sort of synthetic material which can be hardened in the oven, think again. All these synthetic materials contain a softening agent which would enter the body via the lips – not very healthy !

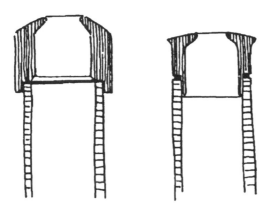

Turned
mouthpieces,
attached
with beeswax.

Turned Didgeridoos

Not many people have the skill or opportunity to turn a didgeridoo; but anyone who can should certainly try it.
If you have any doubts, I would like to mention a few of the advantages. For example, if you are travelling, it is very useful to have a didgeridoo which comes apart. A turned didgeridoo also enables you to make the shape taper more. In Australia these didgeridoos are known as 'malimbas'. In addition, a turned didge does not have a separate mouthpiece, it can all be turned together. In fact, beeswax is a second-best solution.

Even in Australia, it's difficult to find a trunk or branch which is hollowed out so neatly and tapers so precisely that it produces a mouthpiece with exactly the right diameter. The very rare didgeridoos which are made in this way are highly sought after.

Didgeridoos made of Two Pieces

For these didgeridoos, you will need two long pieces of wood sanded into shape. The two pieces must be exactly the same length and, one on top of the other, they should have a square diameter and taper evenly on all sides, rather like an obelisk without a point (see illustration).

Types of wood which are suitable for this are pear, cherry and maple. Alder is also ideal to work with, but does not produce a good resonance. The desired inner diameter is scraped out with a hollow chisel, and any remnants are then polished and removed with sandpaper. It is useful to make a drawing in advance. Using this, you can make stencils to check the diameters both on the inside and the outside of the pipe. As the pipe should taper, it is a good idea to make a large number of stencils with a different diameter so that you have something to compare at every stage of the work.

When both halves have been hollowed out completely smoothly, and exactly the same size, the two halves are glued together with water-resistant glue. The outside is then finished off with a plane, taking care not to go against the grain of the wood. The pipe is then polished with fine sandpaper, and finally it is varnished. The ultimate thickness of the walls of the pipe should be 5 to 10 mm. Using the same method it is possible to make different sorts of instruments, e.g., yidaki, an ordinary didgeridoo and a malimba.

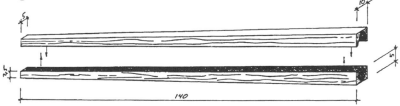

Slidgeridoo / Sliding Didge

Once you have been making your own didgeridoos for a while, you will eventually want to make a telescopic didgeridoo. Charley McMahon is one of the best known musicians to use one of these instruments on the stage.

The principle is the same as the trombone. Notes with a different pitch are produced by changing the length of the pipe. The first difficulty to overcome is finding the right material. The pipes have to work telescopically, i.e., they must fit inside each other with a gap of 1 mm, or at most 2 mm, for the air. It is best to try using an aluminium or a perspex pipe. The knack of building this instrument is to make sure that the pipes can slide one inside the other without any extra air being sucked between the two pipes.

If there is some play between the two pipes, this can be made up with an O-ring. A groove is filed at the end of the thinner pipe and the O-ring is placed in this. (see illustration).

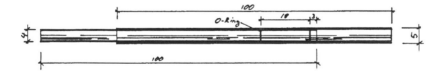

For a perspex inner pipe of 40 mm, use an O-ring with a diameter of 30 mm and a rubber thickness of 2 mm. Try it out and then file it until the groove of the inner pipe is exactly the right depth to ensure that it fits exactly in the outer pipe with the rubber ring (also see illustration on the next page).

However, the two pipes will only slide smoothly once the slidgeridoo has become slightly moist inside with condensed breath.

At the upper end of the outside pipe, i.e., where the inner pipe slides in, a sealing cuff is placed (such as that used in engines) so that the opening is entirely sealed.

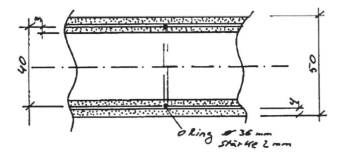

During an interview I asked the leading didgeridoo player, Alan Dargin, what he thought of instruments such as that described above. He grimaced and said that the possibilities of his own didgeridoo were 'by no means exhausted'.

I think it is also a matter of one's approach. In any case, after a few experiments with a few materials and models, I have gone back to my 'natural' didgeridoo. Some things just happen to be good the way they are, and there is no room for technical improvement.

Buying a Didgeridoo

Australia is becoming increasingly popular as a holiday destination. Almost everyone who likes didgeridoos will try to go there and will probably come home with his own didgeridoo. Even if you can't go to Australia, there are increasing possibilities for making a choice nearer home from the growing supplies of this instrument.

Didgeridoos are now often found in music shops, at festivals and at craft fairs; they are increasingly often sold by owners in advertisements or in esoteric journals.

When you buy a didgeridoo, it is obviously best to try it out. If you are not a very good player, it might be best to take along a more experienced player.

The sound is the most important thing, and the way in which it is decorated should always be a secondary consideration.

It may even be that the painting may be a disadvantage: the painting may conceal all sorts of defects. Unfortunately many didgeridoo makers nowadays use a filling knife rather freely. A wooden pipe with holes is no longer simply thrown away, but is neatly filled.

Obviously these repairs are useless after a while because every little crack means that there is a loss of air. There is no proper column of air in the pipe and the sound becomes poorer and poorer. Often the smallest crack may be sufficient to have an adverse effect on the sound.

This does not necessarily mean that the instrument is entirely worthless. Even didgeridoos without fillings sometimes have small cracks.

I have often simply closed these with beeswax, and then the instrument sounded just as good as before.

Larger holes form in a place where there was a branch and where termites have also gnawed in that direction.

If the maker of the didgeridoo wants a beautiful, slender, straight outside at all costs, and smoothes the pipe without looking at these spots, he will usually make a hole in the pipe at this weak point.

Didgeridoos which look rather bendy and knobbly are often a sign that the maker worked really carefully. So it is always a good idea to try out an instrument before buying it.

This also applies to didgeridoos which are curved like a question mark. I don't know why, but usually these curved instruments sound tremendous.

It is a good idea to look inside. Sometimes there are shaving remnants which got stuck on the inside when the outside was sealed. Be careful with these instruments.

In addition, it's possible to see how well the irregularities have been polished inside. Some instruments are improved by being sanded one more time. The thickness of the wall has a great effect on the sound. Pipes made of eucalyptus wood are quite heavy. The thinner the wall, the better the sound, but the sooner they crack.

Didgeridoos which do not need a wax mouthpiece are rare.

It is important to check that the mouthpiece is made of pure beeswax – otherwise you may find that you suffer skin or mouth irritation. It is always possible to replace the mouthpiece yourself.

In some cases, the mouthpiece is kneaded from a black substance. This is not tar, but the wax of wild bees (sugarbacks), which has a wonderfully fragrant smell.

Finally, a few words about the painting. Most didgeridoos are painted with acrylic paints. This has the advantage that the colours are fast. Painting with earth pigments are more original, but they fade fairly quickly.

If you have a didge which is painted with earth pigments, I recommend varnishing it with a thin layer of clear varnish. However, it is a good idea to test it on a small piece first, to avoid any unpleasant surprises.

With all these useful tips, you should not have any problems getting hold of a reasonable didgeridoo.

Appendix

The Map of Australia

Australia is a continent with an area of 7,704,00 square kilometres. Until 1788 this enormous area was populated by dark skinned inhabitants belonging to several different tribes. In 1786, the British government decided that Australia would become the new penal colony for Great Britain, as North America could not longer be used for this purpose after the Declaration of Independence.

On 26 January 1788, a fleet of British ships carrying sailors, officers, convicts and their guards sailed into Botany Bay, the bay where the city of Sydney is now situated.

The original inhabitants have been known as Aborigines ever since, although they obviously called themselves by very different names. They were overwhelmed by the appearance of the white men. At first, they thought that they were the spirits of their ancestors, which is not surprising when you know that an Aborigine's skin becomes lighter as he grows older.

After the first encounter, the arrival of the white men was not very good for the Aborigines. They could not explain that the territorial drive of the invaders completely disrupted the sacred places and the delicate natural balance which they had maintained for thousands of years. The Aborigines soon found themselves in the position of many original inhabitants of 'discovered' countries: that of undesirable, simple nuisances who were, at best, denied their right to self-determination by means of all sorts of oppressive measures, while at worst they were wiped out.

It was only in 1967 that the Aborigines obtained the same legal status as other 'white' Australians. In the meantime, they had

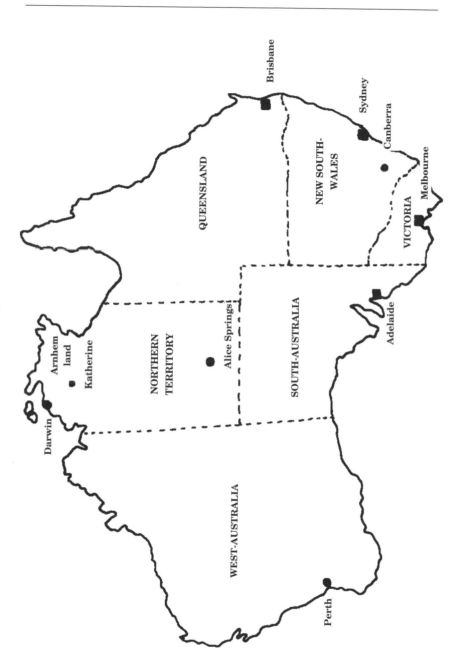

become so uprooted and alienated from their own culture that the social deprivation has by no means ever been compensated. The Aborigines who live in urban areas, far from the roots of their own culture, particularly have problems adapting. Those who have stayed in their own areas and are now living in reserves, for better or worse, are under constant pressure from the threat of the expansion of various mining industries. However, they are generally better off, because despite all their problems, they are better able to live in accordance with their own culture.

Compared with the white population, the Aborigines are on average still far behind at nearly every social level. In general, their housing is poor, as well as the hygiene situation. Infant mortality is high, and children have only a few years of education. Fortunately, bilingual education, with Aboriginal teachers, is gradually developing. At last, the Australian government is introducing aid programmes giving back land, and creating better living conditions to improve the position of the Aborigines.

There is one thing which cannot be returned to them. This concerns the loss of a great deal of their cultural wealth as a result of the destruction of many of their sacred places because of the mining industry and urban development. This means that they can never return to the places where they believe their ancestors are.

The Dreamtime

Once there were about five hundred tribes living in Australia, each with its own version of the creation of the world. Yet there are similarities between them. In all the stories the earth was originally a wild, flat, colourless place where there was no life. There were no people or plants, no animals, no mountains, lakes or rivers. The Great Ancestors or primeval beings slept below the surface of the earth. They looked like animals and plants, but behaved like people. They started moving over the earth so that the sun started to shine, the wind blew and the rain fell.

Looking for food and drink, these great creatures ploughed the earth, creating lakes and mountain chains.

Many version of this story related how the Great Ancestors sang and danced, thus giving life to people, animals and plants. When the work of creation was complete, the Great Ancestors passed the responsibility for maintaining creation to man, and they themselves withdrew to nature. Some became mountains and rivers themselves; others lived on in animals and plants.

Since then, mankind (the Aborigines) have had the sacred task of constantly maintaining creation, for example, by singing the specific songs which relate to particular parts of it. The acts which they perform in this context are still part of the Dreamtime.

Discography

Gary Thomas: Didgeridoo – Ancient Sound of the Future
Aquarius International Music, München

Gary Thomas en Hossam Ramzy: Gaia's Dream
Aquarius International Music, München

Steve Roach , David Hudson, Sandra Hopkins: Australia – Sound of the Earth
Fortuna Records

Tom Wasinger en Jim Harvey: Track to Bumbliwa, a musical journey through the heart of Australia
Silverware Records

Danie Lauter en Suru Ekeh: Ceremony
Raven Recording

Gabriele Roth and the Mirrors: Trance
Raven Recording

Native Ground: One Fine Mama
Raven Recording

Peter Fassbender: Kookaburras Dream – Eine Australische Reise
Peter Fassbender, Wiesbaden

Yothu Yindi: Tribal Voice
    Homeland Movement
    Mushroom Records, Australia

Gondwanaland: Terra Incognita
    Let the dog out
    Wildlife
    Gondwanaland
    Wide Skies
    Warner Music, Australia

Alan Dargin en Michael Atherton: Bloodwood
    Natural Symphonies, Australia

Andrew Langford en Ted Egan: Echos in the Dust
    The original Dreamtime Art Gallery
    PO Box 1655, Alice Springs, NT Australia

David Blanasi: Bamyili Corroboree
    Bamyili Artifacts Group
    (te bestellen bij The original Dreamtime Art Gallery)

George Dreyfus: Sextett for Didgeridoo and Wind Quintett
    EMI Australia

Literature

Maurice Breen: Our Place Our Music, Volume 2
Aboriginal Studies Press, Canberra Australia 1990

Barbara Ann Brennant: Lichtarbeit
Goldmann Verlag, München 1989

John Diamond: Lebensenergie in der Musik
Verlag Bruno Martin, Südergellersen 1990
(Engelse titel: Life Energy in Music)

Ferdinand Dupuis-Panther: Australien
Vsa Verlag, Hamburg 1990

N.H.Fletcher: Acoustics of the Australian didjeridu
Australian Aboriginal Studies, Australia 1983

Stanislaf Grof: Geburt, Tod und Transzendenz
rororo (c) Kösel Verlag, München 1985

Barbara Glowczewski: Träumer der WÜste
Pro Media Verlag

Jennifer Isaacs: Australia's Living Heritage
Ure Smith Press, Sidney 1984

Trevor Jones: The yiraki in north-eastern Arnhemland, Techniques and Styles
uit The Australian Aboriginal Heritage,
Berndt/Philips 1973

Keith Cole: The Aborigines of the Arnhemland
Rigby Limited,
Adelaide/Sydney/Melbourne/Brisbane/Perth
Australia 1979

Wladimir Katchmartchik: Zur Entwicklungsgeschichte der Permanentatmung
Tibia, 18. Jahrgang Heft 1/93, Moeckverlag, Celle

Andrew McMillan: Strict Rules
Hodder & Stoughton, Rydalmere, Australia 1988

Alice M. Moyle: The Australian didjeridu: a late intrusion
World Archaeology Volume 12 no.3 1981

Michael Reimann: Das Didgeridoo
Pan Musikverlag, Zürich 1993 (boek en MC)

Werner Richter: Bewusste Flötentechnik
Musikverlag Zimmermann, Frankfurt a.M. 1986

Bowden Ros en Bill Bunbury: Being Aboriginal
Australian Broadcasting Corporation, Sydney 1990

Brunhilde Sonntag en Renate Matthei: Annäherung V an sieben Komponistinnen
Furore Verlag, Kassel 1989

Wolfgang Strobel: Das Didgeridoo und seine Rolle in der Musiktherapie
Musiktherapeutische Umschau No.13/1992
idem: Klang-Trance-Heilung
Musiktherapeutische Umschau No.9/1988

Peter Sutton: DREAMINGS The Art Of Aboriginal Australia
Viking, Ringwood Vic, Australia 1988

Also published in this series

Eva Rudy Jansen

Singing Bowls

A Practical Handbook of Instruction and Use

Streams of refugees have left Tibet since the Chinese invasion, bringing with them various ritual objects now being sold in the western parts of the world.
Amongst these objects, tho Himalayan singing bowls, also known as Tibetan or Nepalese singing bowls, are a phenomenon which is fascinating more and more people. By going to concerts, undergoing so-called 'sound-massages', listening to soundrecords and by experimenting themselves, people discover all sorts of possibilities and aspects of the special, singing sound of the metal bowls.

This book explores these possibilities and aspects, and tells something about the backgrounds; covering a wide range of items such as the meeting between East and West, sacrificial dishes, secret and lost knowledge, shamanism, as well as scientific phenomena like synchronization and brainwaves.
Although the short scope of the book won't provide absolute answers to all the questions you may have about the bowls, it certainly does provide practical information about how to start exploring this fascinating world of sound yourself and how to go about finding the bowl that is right for you.

The book also contains an extra chapter describing three other ritual objects: tingshaws (small cymbals), dorje (thunderbolt) and bell.

ISBN 90-74597-01-7

Eva Rudy Jansen

The Book of Buddhas

Ritual Symbolism used on
Buddhist Statuary and Ritual Objects

Modern students who are drawn to the study and practice of
Buddhism, as well as anyone else with an interest in this field,
are not always able to easily learn the symbolic meaning of the
various types of statuary connected to the study of this
philosophy or presented to us in musea and an increasing
numbers of stores selling Asian artefacts.
In Buddhism, every symbol has a meaning, and this book
explores the symbolism of the ritual objects that are used on
statues and paintings, as well as explaining the ritual meaning
of the objects associated with Buddhism. The book is not a
comprehensive and exhausting study, but it provides an
introduction to Buddhism itself, as well as a generous survey in
words and images of the most common figures, positions and
symbols in Mahayana and Tantrayana Buddhism.
The author examines the Three Mysteries, mudras, asananas,
Manushri Buddhas, Transcendental Buddhas, Adibuddha,
Tara, Boddhisattva's (i.e. Avalokiteshvara), as well als Yidams,
Gods and Goddesses, dakinis and yoginis, and the so-called
Laughing Buddha.
Each individual item is clearly illustrated and accompanied by
a short description of its significance. An index is added for easy
reference.

ISBN 90-74597-02-5

Eva Rudy Jansen
The Book of Hindu Imagery
The Gods and their Symbols

Hinduism is more than a religion; it is a way of life that has developed over approximately 5 millennia. Its rich and multicultured history, which has no equivalent among the great religions of the world, has made the structure of its mythical and philosophical principles into a highly differentiated maze, of which total knowledge is a practical impossibility.

This volume cannot offer a complete survey of the meaning of Hinduism, but Eva Rudy Jansen does provide an extensive compilation of important deities and their divine manifestations, so that modern students and anyone else who has an interest in Hinduism, can understand the significance of the Hindu pantheon.
To facilitate easy recognition, a survey of ritual gestures, postures, attires and attributes as well as an index are included.

Over 100 illustrations and several photographs make this book an important reference, both to the student of Hindu art and the interested amateur.

ISBN 90-74597-07-6 PBk.
ISBN 90-74597-10-6 cloth

Ab Williams

The Complete Book of Chinese Health Balls

Backgroud and Use of the Health Balls

Reduce stress!
Learn Meridian Ball Therapy

Do you own a set of Chinese Health Balls? Known as
Boading balls, **Baud** balls, or just health balls, they're
certainly much more than a curio! People have been using
them for centuries. The balls are explained, exercises are
included, the treatments revealed – here, for the first time!
More and more people in the West are looking for answers in
Eastern medicine, lifestyle and therapies. Just about everyone
has heard of **yoga, meditation, acupuncture.** This book is
aimed at drawing your attention to the still relatively
unknown phenomenon of Chinese Health Balls.
Step by step, you can practice the many exercises to master
Meridian Ball Therapy, a therapy that can make a significant
contribution to your physical and spiritual health!

ISBN 90-74597-28-9

Töm Klöwer

The Joy of Drumming

Drums en Percussion Instruments from around the World

If you think you're not musical, think again! Rhythm, the foundation of music, is all around and within us. In the womb, we began our experience of the world through the sounds of our mother's hearbeat and the cadence of her voice. Experiencing rhythm and movement is an essential part of healthy living, and Töm Klöwer shows you how to reconnect with this life-affirming energy. Within these pages you're sure to find at least one instrument that will get you resonating, and once you do, you can work with the simple rhythm exercises Klöwer presents to begin your journey into the world of drumming.

The book includes over *100 illustrations of different drums, gongs, and sound effect instruments,* along with descriptions of how they are made, and basic playing techniques. From the most ancient instruments to the most modern inventions, from *Asia, Australia, Africa, and South America,* one of these instruments is sure to capture your imagination.

For more advanced drummers, Klöwer presents traditional rhythm patterns from Africa and South America, and music therapists will be inspired by the broad range of instruments he describes. His exercises can be performed by an individuel as well as a group of people.

ISBN 90-74597-13-9

George Hulskramer

The Life of Buddha

From Prince Siddhartha to Buddha

There are few histories of Prince Siddhartha that are as
accessible to all ages as this one. In comic-book format,
Hulskramer tells the colorful story of the Buddha Siddhartha,
skillfully illustrated by Nepalese artists Raju Babu Shakya and
Bijay Raj Shakya. This is a readable biography for anyone who
is intrested in Buddhism, a wonderful, exotic fairy for lovers of
beautiful illustrated stories, and a collector's item for cartoon
enthusiasts. 72 pp.

ISBN 90-74597-17-3